SHADOW INTO SUNLIGHT

Other Books by Elaine Shelabarger

First Love, Last Love
Shadows of the Past

SHADOW INTO SUNLIGHT

•

Elaine Shelabarger

AVALON BOOKS

NEW YORK

Published by Avalon Books,
an imprint of Thomas Bouregy & Co., Inc.
New York, NY

Library of Congress Cataloging-in-Publication Data

Shelabarger, Elaine.
  Shadow into sunlight / Elaine Shelabarger.
      p. cm.
  ISBN 978-0-8034-7472-7 (hardcover : acid-free paper)
  1. Young women—Fiction.   2. English—Italy—Fiction.
3. Love stories. gsafd   I. Title.
  PS3619.H4522S47 2012
  813'.6—dc23
                                        2011042145

PRINTED IN THE UNITED STATES OF AMERICA
ON ACID-FREE PAPER
BY RR DONNELLEY, HARRISONBURG, VIRGINIA

For Leah, my darling granddaughter,
with my love

Prologue

He had walked the mean streets for an hour before he found the place he was looking for. As he mounted the flight of ramshackle iron steps, he was conscious of the hostile stares of the men lounging at the side of the tenement building.

It was not the safest place for a young man of his class to be, particularly at this time of day, with dusk falling fast, and he knew it. But he had come here for a reason, and nothing would deter him from his purpose.

He had knocked with his ebony-headed cane several times on the blistered wood of the front door before it opened a few inches and he found himself looking down into the eyes of a child.

"Mother is sick, sir," she said politely. "I am sorry, but she will not see anyone."

The little girl could not have been more than nine or ten years old, he thought. She was painfully thin, her pale hair caught back from her pinched white face, her cotton gown clean but threadbare. The blue eyes were fearful, but there was courage in the determined set of her chin.

He smiled at her. "I think she will see me," he said gently, and he held out his card. "Give her this."

When he entered the dingy, low-ceilinged room, the woman sitting at the scrubbed wooden table got quickly to her feet. As she did so, she was racked with a painful cough and pressed a handkerchief to her lips. She was wearing a shabby gray gown and had wrapped a shawl around her frail shoulders. There were great, dark shadows beneath her eyes, and she was as thin and pale and fragile as her daughter. But she faced the visitor with the same quiet dignity and courage.

"I do not know what you want of me, sir," she said quietly. "But I assure you, I have nothing left to give."

He did not need to be told that. Apart from the table and two broken-backed chairs, the only furniture in the room was a rickety cupboard and, in a dark corner, an iron bedstead covered by a worn quilt. The fireplace was empty despite the chill of the October evening, and on the table were the meager remains of a stale loaf and a bowl of what appeared to be gruel.

He stood there for a few moments in shocked silence, dry-mouthed and quite unable to frame the words he had so carefully rehearsed.

"I am sorry, ma'am. I had no idea it had come to this," he said at last.

She looked at him in utter despair. "Please go," she said brokenly. "I have nothing to say to you—nothing that has not already been said."

As she succumbed to another bout of coughing, the child went to her side and put her little arms around her waist.

"If my pa was here," she said with a fierce glance at the visitor, "he would get Mother some linctus for her cough."

"Hush, Rachel!"

The young man flinched at the look of pain on the woman's face, and over the child's head his eyes pleaded with her.

"You must see a doctor!" He made no attempt to mask the depth of his feelings. "Let me help you! It is the least I can do."

She shook her head. "I want nothing from you."

"Please!" His voice was desperate. "It is the only way in which I can express my deep regret for what has happened."

The tired blue eyes were filled with scorn. "You expect me to help you relieve your feelings of guilt?"

His hands clenched on his cane. "That is not possible," he said harshly. "I shall carry those with me for the rest of my life."

In the painful silence, Rachel left her mother's side and took his hand. "Ma doesn't mean it," she said, gazing up at him imploringly. "Please, help to make her better."

He looked down at the child with gratitude and relief. "I will return with my carriage within the hour," he said to them. "Please be ready to go with me."

And without another word, he turned and hurried from the dismal room.

Chapter One

Europe
1870

The evening sun was still fierce when Lucy Ashleigh stepped out onto her balcony overlooking the beautiful city of Florence. The views from the Castello were breathtaking.

Perched on a green hillside high above the River Arno, it had been the home of the di Lorenzos for generations, and Lucy had been spending the summer here, in this beautiful part of Tuscany, with her Italian cousins.

It was her first visit to the Castello, and despite the warmth of the welcome she had received and the beauty of her surroundings, she was now secretly looking forward to her return to England in September. Much as she had enjoyed getting to know the Italian branch of her family, she had begun to ache for a glimpse of her beloved home in the Devonshire village of Lintern Magna. Today, she thought with a sigh, she would have given a great deal to exchange the harsh glare of the sun on that glittering Florentine landscape for a rainy afternoon in an English meadow.

Normally, before dinner, she would have spent a little while strolling in the shady gardens under the cypress trees with her cousin Sofia and practicing her Italian. Sofia's governess was from London, and, as a result, her English was fluent. She enjoyed teasing Lucy about her accent, which, to her delight, was steadily improving. But tonight, her great-grandmother, the

Contessa di Lorenzo, was holding a soiree, and it was time to summon her maid to help her dress.

She turned back into her richly decorated room, with its magnificent four-poster bed and vivid blue hangings, and opened the shutters a little to let in some light. With its ornately carved oak furniture and the elegant chaise longue piled with velvet cushions of pale gold, it had been her sanctuary for the past months. It was here that she had wept homesick tears when she had first arrived, here that she had written tearful letters to her stepmother. And where at last she had begun to smile again and enjoy all that the Castello and Florence had to offer.

She crossed the room and looked at herself in the gilt-framed cheval mirror. Her cheeks had lost the pallor of the first weeks of her arrival, when she had felt as if her entire world had come crashing down around her. The dark eyes inherited from her Italian grandmother had regained their sparkle, and her creamy skin was lit as if from within by a soft, luminous glow.

Her parents, she thought, had been right to send her here, to Florence, although at first she had been loath to leave Ashleigh Manor and the comforts of home. First love, her stepmother, Adeline Ashleigh, had explained, could be extremely painful, especially when it ended unhappily. But she had promised her that, given time and distance, the heartache would diminish. And she had been quite right. Lucy's visit had done much to help heal her bruised heart. She thought about James Wyatt less and less with every day that went by, and although she was still finding it hard to put the whole humiliating episode behind her, she had slowly begun to realize that it was quite possible, after all, to be happy once again.

As Loretta, her little Florentine maid, helped her to step into her dress, Lucy reminded herself how fortunate she was to be here at the Castello. Ten years ago, lost and destitute, struggling each day for survival, she could never have dreamed of this wonderful place.

The circumstances of her birth had meant that she had been

denied a conventional upbringing. Lucy had been born while her father was abroad. And her mother had died tragically before being able to tell her young husband of his daughter's existence.

Lucy had bravely endured ten years of suffering in a work-house—a soulless and cruel English institution used by politicians to solve the problem of poverty—before the truth of her background came to light. It was through the lady who was now her beloved stepmother, and whom she also considered her dearest friend, that she and her father had found each other.

She must never allow herself to forget how blessed she was, she told herself. And tonight, she would smile and mingle with the guests and please her great-grandmother, who had welcomed her into her ancestral home and made her feel that she was a valued member of the family.

When they had first met, the dignified old lady had taken Lucy's face in her tiny, wrinkled hands and pronounced that she was the living image of her father.

"I wish for you to enjoy your time here in Firenze," she had told her in her correct but heavily accented English. "But I must insist on your respect for the rules of our society while you are under my roof and in my guardianship."

"Of course, Great-Grandmother."

"I do not know what is expected of you in England, but in Italy a lady must behave always in a seemly manner. Modesty and meekness are essential at all times. Also, you will never venture out into the streets alone, and of course there will be no contact with a gentleman unless you are chaperoned. I hope that is understood, *cara mia*?"

Lucy nodded. "That is exactly what would be expected of me at home."

She had seen little of the Contessa during her stay, but like everyone else at the Castello, she was always aware of her formidable presence. At the age of eighty, with her immaculately coiffed silver hair and proud, aristocratic face, she still ruled her large family with a rod of iron, and they were all in awe of her. Tonight, Lucy thought, she would be expected to look her best. Her great-grandmother would preside over the proceedings with her usual air of complete command, and she would, of course, be running a critical eye over the dress and behavior of Sofia and Lucy, the two youngest members of the family.

"*Bellissima!*" Loretta clapped her hands in delight as she stepped back to survey her young mistress, and Lucy smiled, blushing at the artless compliment.

Normally, she preferred to see to her own toilette, but tonight, on this glamorous occasion, she had decided that she needed her maid. She was wearing the white tulle dress her stepmother had helped her to choose in London for just this sort of event. The full skirt touched the ground, and the close-fitting embroidered bodice emphasized the slenderness of her figure. Her silky dark hair was piled high with soft curls, and she wore a narrow satin ribbon around her graceful neck. Her only jewelry was a ring set with rubies and emeralds that had once belonged to her mother. It had been given to her two years ago, on her eighteenth birthday, by her father.

With a last, swift glance in the mirror, Lucy took her lace fan from Loretta, left her room, and made her way calmly enough down the Long Gallery past the ancestral portraits of the di Lorenzos gazing down impassively at her from the paneled walls. But as she reached the head of the Grand Staircase and looked down at the glittering array of Italian nobility below her on the marble-floored mezzanine, her nerves almost got the better of her.

At home, the social occasions she normally attended took place among people she knew—or at least, those with whom she had a passing acquaintance. But here, apart from the immediate members of the family and their friends, she was a stranger among a bewildering congregation of rich and fashionable people she had never met before. And for a breathless moment, she longed to turn and run back to the safety of her room.

Then, reminding herself that her father would expect her to behave in a manner becoming her proud ancestry, she took a deep, calming breath, held up her head, and began to descend the stairs.

It was as she reached the last steps that the heel of her slipper caught in the hem of her dress. She swayed perilously, snatching at air. Just before she toppled forward, she suddenly felt herself seized around the waist by a pair of strong hands and deposited, with her balance, if not her dignity, intact, at the bottom of the stairs.

It was done so adroitly and with such speed that it scarcely drew attention. In any case, the surge of relief she felt had rendered her blind to the curious looks of those who had noticed.

She caught her breath as the tall, fair-haired man who had come so swiftly to her rescue took her hand to support her while he bent down and quickly freed the heel of her slipper.

"Mille grazie, Signore!"

Lucy looked up, blushing, into eyes of an extraordinary pale blue. She and her rescuer gazed at each other. For the space of a heartbeat, time stopped.

Then, with a graceful bow, he bent over her hand. *"Signorina."*

And he was gone, disappearing among the throng of guests making their way toward the *salotto.*

She was not Italian, despite her sloe black eyes and the sheen of her dark hair. Major Charles Ryman was certain of that. That exquisitely delicate skin could not have achieved such perfection under the glare of the hot Florentine sun. And her accent had confirmed that, like himself, she was foreign. From where he was standing, in a window recess, he could see her mingling with the guests. And judging from her shy smile and her quiet, reserved manners, he surmised that she was probably English.

He cursed himself for failing to take advantage of the opportunity to make her acquaintance. That moment near the staircase, when their eyes had met! It had been like gazing into the sun. And, as if dazzled by the brightness, he had foolishly averted his eyes and walked away.

Charles was surprised by his unusually gauche behavior. He had been traveling the Continent for the past six months, trying, as usual, to escape his demons and using, in his search for peace of mind and happiness, his very considerable means to move in the most cultivated milieu in the whole of Europe. He had spent time in the company of many beautiful and elegant women—women who made no secret of their interest in him. Their appeal, however, had been superficial, and his heart had remained intact.

But tonight, he had looked into the eyes of a young, unsophisticated girl, had held her, for a fleeting moment, in his arms, and had felt his jaded senses quicken into life. The sensation had taken him by surprise, and the suddenness of it had been alarming.

"She is charming, is she not?" Count Eduardo Ortalli, who had been standing with folded arms, silently observing his friend, raised a quizzical eyebrow.

"Whom do you mean?" Charles assumed a carefully blank expression.

Eduardo laughed. "Do not imagine, Charles, that you can fool an old friend. You have been staring at the beautiful English *signorina* all evening. I do not blame you. But if you wish to make her acquaintance, you had better hurry. She will be leaving Florence to return to her home in a few weeks."

Charles shrugged carelessly. "Really? Who is she, anyway?"

"Her name is Lucy Ashleigh. Her grandmother was a di Lorenzo—the youngest daughter of the Contessa. She married an Englishman, and they died young, in tragic circumstances. Their only child—the *signorina's* father—was born and brought up in England."

So he had been right, Charles thought. Although there was Italian blood flowing in her veins, Miss Ashleigh was essentially an English rose. An interesting combination!

"Come," Eduardo said, taking his elbow. "Let me put you out of your misery and introduce you to the young lady."

But Charles shook him off. "Later, perhaps."

Something was telling him that meeting Miss Ashleigh might be a significant moment—perhaps one of the most significant moments of his life. And he was not at all certain that he should allow himself the pleasure.

Eduardo was puzzled. It was not like Charles to refuse an opportunity to meet a beautiful woman. Ladies were invariably attracted to him—he was extremely good-looking, wealthy, and well-informed, and his distinguished military background added to his mystique. Charles had led a cavalry charge at Gettysburg, where he had been wounded, and he had been awarded the Medal of Honor for conspicuous gallantry. He had been destined for high rank but had left the regular service to join the Reserve and, following his father's death, had inherited Rymans, the family business.

Eduardo had met him two years ago when the well-known firm had begun doing business with the Ortallis, importing their goods—mainly *objets d'art* and Italian antiques—to New York. But although the two men had become friends, they were not close, and Eduardo knew very little about his personal life.

He was, of course, aware that Charles did not suffer fools gladly and that there were times when he withdrew entirely from the social whirl, times when there was something in his expression that made Eduardo wonder whether, beneath the poised, rather remote manner, there was some deep personal sadness he kept strictly to himself. Perhaps, Eduardo thought, he was lonely, and it was time that he settled for marriage with one of the accomplished and beautiful women who frequently set their caps at him.

Now, watching him bend, with consummate gallantry, over the hand of a handsome but aging marchesa, Eduardo decided that perhaps it was best that Charles kept his distance from the English girl. She must be at least ten years younger than he and would quickly find herself out of her depth with a man of his experience. No, he thought, perhaps he should not go out of his way to make the introduction. Lucy Ashleigh was both sweet and innocent, and he did not wish to see her hurt.

"Who is the tall, fair-haired man standing near the window?" Lucy whispered to her cousin Sofia behind her fan, careful to keep her voice down. The Contessa was watching for signs of inappropriate behavior and had already rebuked them for speaking too loudly.

"You mean the one talking to my cousin Eduardo?" Sofia gave her a mischievous smile. "He is very handsome, is he not?"

"Very."

With his lion mane of gold-blond hair combined with an almost regal bearing, he had the kind of distinctive good looks that turned heads in a crowd. The nose was aquiline above a chiseled mouth, and his skin had the healthy glow of a man who spent a great deal of time out of doors.

"His name is Major Charles Ryman," Sofia murmured. "And he is an American."

"Really? How interesting!" Why, Lucy wondered, was her heart suddenly beating a little faster? "I have never met anyone from America."

Sofia giggled. "And you are not likely to either if Great-Grandmama has anything to do with it! They say he is a dreadful flirt and that half the ladies in Florence are in love with him. Naturally, she disapproves. I heard her telling my uncle that he should not have been included on the guest list."

"Heavens!" Lucy looked suitably horrified, but Sofia's remarks had merely increased her interest. Certainly, she was not the only woman in the room whose attention he had attracted. His looks were, after all, extremely striking, but she was fairly certain that Major Ryman had not flirted with anyone that evening. To her certain knowledge, he hadn't moved from his position by the window. The only person she had seen him in conversation with, apart from Count Eduardo Ortalli, had been a rather frail old lady.

Besides, his manner, when he had come so gallantly to her rescue on the stairs, had been perfectly formal and correct. But she had noticed, once or twice, that he had been looking in her direction—although that might, of course, have been her imagination.

Sofia's round black eyes were sparkling wickedly. "Look,"

she whispered, "Great-Grandmama is going outside to the loggia—probably for some air. She's been complaining that it is too hot for her among all these people. Now is your chance!"

"What do you mean?" Lucy looked at her cousin nervously.

"To meet Major Ryman, of course!" Sofia took her hand. "Come. I've been meaning to talk to Eduardo all evening, and I'm certain he will be delighted to introduce us to his friend."

"Sofia, wait!"

But, to Lucy's embarrassment, her cousin took her arm very firmly and propelled her across the room toward the two men.

"*Buona sera,* Eduardo!" Sofia said with a coquettish smile. "Why have you not been to see us lately? We have missed you very much!"

"Sofia!" He kissed her formally on both cheeks and made Lucy a graceful bow. "Did the Contessa not tell you? I have been traveling on business with my friend Charles. Let me introduce you both."

"Charles, may I present Signorina Sofia di Lorenzo and her cousin, Miss Lucy Ashleigh? Ladies, allow me to introduce my friend Major Charles Ryman."

Lucy felt the color mounting in her cheeks as the Major bowed over her hand.

"Miss Ashleigh and I," he said, his mouth relaxing into a smile, "met very briefly on the stairs earlier."

"Really?" Sofia raised an eyebrow at her cousin. "So that is why she wished to know who you were!" she said with a tactless smile.

There was a pause, and Lucy felt the color flood into her face. Major Ryman must have noticed her embarrassment, because he turned and spoke to her in English, his voice gentle. "I hope," he said, "that I didn't damage the hem of your dress. I'm afraid I might have been rather clumsy."

"No, not at all," Lucy said, rather breathlessly. "I was most grateful for your help."

"It was entirely my pleasure, ma'am." The deep voice, with its distinctive American accent, seemed to her utterly charming.

She raised her eyes to his and was once again struck by their compelling beauty. They had the color of the sea in them, she thought distractedly, and their expression, as he smiled at her, suffused her suddenly with warmth.

"So you have been spending the summer here in Florence," he said. "It is a beautiful city, don't you think?"

"Yes, indeed," she murmured. "The architecture is quite wonderful, and there is so much to see."

Sofia laughed. "The English—they are all the same!" she announced disparagingly. "If they could, they would spend every moment sightseeing under the hot sun!"

"Isn't that rather the purpose of visiting Italy?" Charles Ryman asked her dryly.

Sofia laughed, not at all put out by his tone. "I am afraid that old buildings bore me terribly! But my cousin adores them, so I am quite happy to accompany her on all her little excursions. What brings you here, Major Ryman—business or pleasure?"

"Both. Personally, I never tire of Florence." He turned to Lucy. "The Duomo, for example, must be one of the finest cathedrals in the whole of Europe. Don't you agree, Miss Ashleigh?"

"Oh, yes, I'm sure it must be!" For a moment, her shyness left her. "And I love the views from the Piazza Michelangelo."

"They are magnificent. I was there only yesterday."

"They say it is the best vantage point in the area."

"I believe it is!" Major Ryman's blue eyes were studying Lucy's face with frank interest. "Have you been in Florence long, Miss Ashleigh?"

"Since April. This is my first visit to Italy."

"And have you seen much of the countryside?"

"A little. But not as much as I would have liked."

"Then it is time we remedied that!" Eduardo said, smiling at her. "Why don't you and Sofia come and visit me at my house in San Matteo? I'm going there myself tomorrow, and if you wish, you could both accompany me. It's a delightful drive— only eight kilometers—and it means that you will see some of our beautiful Tuscan countryside. What do you say, ladies? I promise you, I will do my utmost to make you both welcome."

Sofia clapped her hands! *"Eccellente!* I adore your wonderful house, Eduardo. We would love to go with you, would we not, Lucy?"

"Yes, indeed. Thank you so much for the kind invitation."

Eduardo bowed. "I look forward to the occasion."

"You will fall in love with the Villa San Matteo, I promise you!" Sofia said. "Have you visited my cousin there, Major Ryman?"

"Not recently."

Sofia darted a triumphant glance at her cousin. "Then," she said, smiling up at him, "why not join us?"

Lucy looked away quickly, horrified by her cousin's shameless maneuvering.

"Of course, Charles, why not?" Eduardo said, his dark eyes amused. "I'm sure the ladies would enjoy your company. Are you free tomorrow?"

Lucy felt his eyes upon her, brilliantly blue and sparkling.

"I have an early appointment in the morning," he said. "And I am not sure when it will finish. But, thank you. I may join you later."

Chapter Two

"Sofia, how could you!" Lucy had been obliged to wait until the soiree was over and the guests had left before she had a chance to speak to her cousin alone.

"*Mi scusi?*" Sofia assumed an expression of complete innocence. "What is it that I have done?"

"You know quite well that you deliberately contrived to have Major Ryman invited to the Villa San Matteo!"

"Pouf! What if I did? He seemed delighted with the idea. And you know perfectly well you would like to get to know him better. Why did you not tell me you had already met?"

"We hadn't—not really. He . . . helped me when I caught my heel in the hem of my dress, that is all."

Sofia sighed. "*Romantico!*" She clasped her hands together rapturously. "You see? It is all meant to be! You will be grateful to me one day, I promise you. It is time you forgot all about that miserable James. And Major Ryman will help you to do so!"

Lucy sighed. Sometimes, she wished that she had not confided in Sofia. She had grown fond of her cousin, but she was not entirely certain that she could rely upon her discretion. "You must not call James 'miserable.' What happened was not his fault. He could not have defied his parents, and I would never have wanted him to."

Sofia shrugged her shoulders eloquently. "Believe what you wish, *cara*, but please, try to forget the past. Instead, think only of the delights in store for you tomorrow in the company of the charming and handsome Major Ryman."

"You talk such nonsense!" Lucy shook her head. "The

Contessa will never allow us to go, when she knows he might be there."

Sofia laughed. "I have already told her about the invitation, and she was happy for us to accept. You see, I know that she is hoping that, one day, Eduardo and I might be a little closer than distant cousins. We won't, of course. I am very fond of him, but I would not marry him if he were the last man on earth." Her eyes glittered with mischief. "But I see no need to tell her that just yet!"

"And she really doesn't mind that Major Ryman will be there as well?

"My dearest cousin, you are such an innocent. Do you know, I quite forgot to mention his name!"

Lucy went to her room with her mind spinning. Sofia was right: she really was an innocent. In terms of worldliness and sophistication, her cousin was very far in advance, although she was fully a year younger. Perhaps, she thought, as Loretta helped her take off her finery, it was because Sofia had grown up in a large family of older brothers and sisters and had no doubt learned her worldly ways from them. Lucy was an eldest child. Her half brothers, Harry and Piers, were still little boys, and Antonia, the youngest member of the family, was only three years old.

She missed them all, she suddenly realized, with an ache far greater than she would have thought possible. Far more, in fact, than she missed James, although it was still painful to remember how deeply his letter had hurt her. It had been so completely unexpected. Her life had been mapped out before her—or so she had believed. Marriage to the boy she had loved since she was a child, a beautiful home near her beloved parents, children they would both cherish. A tranquil, ordered existence, and, just as the best stories always ended, happiness ever after. She had never imagined that suddenly, without warning, her innocent hopes would be so cruelly dashed.

The letter she had received from James on that cold November morning was locked in her bureau at home, together with the few small keepsakes he had given her. Not that she had needed to keep it; the formal, stilted words were forever etched into her memory.

My dearest Lucy,

I hope you will not think too badly of me for what I am about to say. This is the most difficult letter I have ever had to write, but I have no other choice.

My parents have informed me that they are utterly opposed to a match between us and have forbidden me to approach your father.

I will not elaborate upon the reasons for their objection, apart from stating that they deem your background unsuitable. My father has made it clear that if I defy him, he will immediately withdraw my allowance and alter the terms of his Will in my brother's favor.

After careful consideration, I feel that I have no alternative but to withdraw my offer of marriage, much as it pains me to do so.

Please believe me when I say how utterly wretched I feel. I pray that you can find it in your heart to forgive me.

With my deepest regrets and most affectionate wishes, And believe me,

Yours most devotedly,
James Wyatt

She might have taken it better if he'd had the courage to come to speak to her in person. The pain of the rejection had been a cruel reminder of the suffering she had endured in her early childhood. Thanks to the love and care lavished upon her by her father and stepmother, she had been able to put the past behind her. And, perhaps rather foolishly, she had never imagined that it might influence her adult life.

She and James had been fond of each other since they had first met, when Lucy was barely eleven years old and he just two years older. Both belonged to old, established families in the neighborhood, and their lives had become happily and inextricably entwined.

They had planned to announce their engagement when James attained his majority on his twenty-first birthday on Christmas Eve of last year. Instead, he and his parents had left Lintern Magna to share the celebration with relatives in Norfolk. And despite the best efforts of family and friends to comfort and sustain her, the festive season seemed to pass Lucy by. Although she had said very little, she had suffered greatly. She had not only lost her sweetheart but had been forced to endure the pain of a very public humiliation. The Wyatts had made no secret of their part in it, and for some time, the entire neighborhood had been a hotbed of gossip.

Lucy's father was furiously angry at the Wyatts' treatment of his beloved daughter.

"If the truth be known, the boy is not good enough for her!" Guy Ashleigh had raged. "And I've a mind to go and make my feelings known to the Wyatts and that cowardly young whelp of theirs!"

But her stepmother, who had once herself been the unhappy subject of gossip and rumor, held him back.

"It is best left, my love. If you intervene, you will only add fuel to the flames," Adeline said. "Lucy is young. She will come to see that she deserves better. And one day she will find a young man who will make her as happy as you have made me!"

But as winter melted into spring, her parents had begun to be extremely concerned about the quiet little figure that flitted, specter-like, about the house. It was Adeline who had suggested a visit to Florence, and by a happy coincidence, Jane Ambrose and her sister, both friends of the family, were also planning to visit Italy. Accordingly, arrangements were made for Lucy to travel with them.

Lucy sighed, remembering her mood of despondency as she had left England. The events of the evening had somehow unsettled her, bringing thoughts that she believed she had left behind.

"You have had a pleasant evening, *signorina*?" Loretta,

watching her in the mirror as she removed the hairpins and brushed out Lucy's silky, waist-length hair, had noted her troubled expression.

She forced herself back to the present and smiled. "Thank you, yes. Most pleasant."

Resolutely, she forced herself to concentrate on what she would wear for the following day's visit to the Villa San Matteo and was immediately assailed by a fluttering of butterflies in the pit of her stomach.

Perhaps, she thought, Major Ryman really would be joining them. If he was as notorious as the Contessa believed him to be, he was the very last person her parents would want her to associate with. But she had never before met anyone remotely like him, and she could not deny that she had found him fascinating. In fact, the very thought of him seemed to dispel the shadows that still haunted her past.

After Loretta had said good night and left her, Lucy threw open the French doors and went to stand on the balcony, looking in her white lace peignoir, like a sleepy ghost as she breathed in the soft night air. Below her, the city of Florence slept under a myriad of bright stars, and the scent of orange blossoms hung upon the light breeze.

Only a few hours ago, she had been standing here on this very spot, thinking longingly of home. And now, Florence seemed to her to be the most exciting and desirable place in the entire world.

Her last waking thought as she lay in her bed between the silk sheets was the pleasant prospect of the day ahead. Tomorrow, perhaps, she might be seeing Major Ryman again.

At eleven o'clock the following morning, Count Eduardo Ortalli presented himself at the Castello and escorted the two young ladies to his landau, which was waiting in the courtyard in the dazzling sunshine.

"I have left the hood down, so that your view will not be obstructed," Eduardo said, as they admired the elegant vehicle.

It was the very latest model, held four passengers, and was pulled by four smart grays. "But please, tell me if the sun becomes too hot."

Lucy had dressed carefully for the occasion and wore a wide-brimmed straw bonnet trimmed with a satin ribbon and a dress of fine pink lawn with short, puffed sleeves. She looked, she thought, very English.

Sofia was wearing green, trimmed with gold, which enhanced her vivid Italian coloring.

"There is nothing I like better than to feel the cool air on my face," Sophia said, with a sigh of satisfaction as the groom flicked the reins and they began to move off. "I am so looking forward to the drive!"

"My friend Charles hopes to arrive in time for luncheon," Eduardo explained, and the meaningful sidelong glance Sofia darted at Lucy made her look away in confusion. If this was the indiscreet manner in which her cousin intended to behave, she thought, it would have been better to have declined the invitation.

"Tell me," Sofia asked with an innocent smile, "have you known Major Ryman long, Eduardo?"

"Two years, perhaps. Since Rymans began to do business with the family firm.

"They say he is quite a favorite with the ladies," Sofia said, with a mischievous glance at her cousin, who was staring straight ahead with a fixed smile.

Eduardo shrugged. "Perhaps because of his distinguished military background. He was wounded in one of the major battles of the American Civil War and was decorated for gallantry. He refuses to talk about his experiences, although I have tried to draw him out on many an occasion."

"How thrilling! Don't you think so, Lucy?"

"Yes, indeed." She shot her cousin an annoyed glance. There were times when her teasing went too far.

To her relief, Sofia soon turned her attention to Eduardo, and Lucy began to enjoy the carriage ride through the rolling Tuscan countryside, with its pine-shaded olive groves and its orchards laden with peaches and cherries. They passed ancient farmhouses guarded by tall cypress trees, and shy peasant children waved at them as they passed along the dusty white road.

"You must find a great contrast between our sun-baked landscape and your green English countryside," Eduardo remarked to her as the carriage swayed over the uneven road.

"Oh, indeed." She smiled. "But each is beautiful in its own way." And once again, she was suddenly homesick for the wooded valleys and the wild, windswept uplands of Dartmoor.

"We will soon be there." Eduardo pointed ahead to a thicket of stunted olive trees on the brow of a gentle hill. They drove through tall iron gates and down a long, curved avenue of cypress trees, and then the groom pulled up outside the beautiful fifteenth-century façade of the Villa San Matteo.

Eduardo was pleased by Lucy's interest in its graceful architecture.

"It was once a Benedictine monastery," he explained. "It came into my family almost two hundred years ago. Later, I will show you the gardens. But, first, refreshment, I think!" He led the way to a colonnaded terrace and seated them at a marble-topped table set among huge stone urns bright with cyclamen and bougainvillea

They had just been served tall glasses of lemon cordial when there came the sound of rapid hoofbeats. Lucy's heart suddenly leaped into her throat at the sight of the horseman astride a handsome chestnut mare. He swung down with easy grace from the saddle and handed the reins to the groom. Then, doffing his hat, Charles Ryman hurried up the steps to the terrace and strode toward them.

What was there about this man, Lucy wondered, as, after a tour of the magnificently appointed house, they sat over lunch, served al fresco in the cool shade of the loggia.

Normally, Lucy found the long, five-course midday meal with its confusing array of cold meats and strongly flavored dishes rather too rich for her English tastes. She had never before sampled black truffles or anchovies until she had been served them at the Castello, and she had decided she liked neither. But today she was hardly aware of what she was eating.

Again and again, she had been forced to remind herself not to stare at Major Ryman. How alien he appeared against this extravagant Italian setting! There was a glamour about him that had nothing to do with his good looks and tall stature. Replace his elegant English riding clothes with a Cavalry uniform, and then, she thought, he would be truly in his element—at home in a landscape of rugged mountains and deep valleys where men rode hard under the high blue dome of the open sky.

Suddenly aware that the subject of her imagination was observing her with great interest over the rim of his glass, she hastened to cover her confusion.

"Have you lived in New York City all your life, Major Ryman?" she asked him diffidently.

"For much of it. My father moved the family there to go into business with a relative when I was a boy. But I was born in a small township in the Mohawk Valley near Fort Hunter."

"Heavens! Red Indians!" Sofia, wide-eyed, covered her lips with her fingers.

He smiled. "Fifty years ago, there were ten thousand of the tribe living in the area. But the smallpox and other diseases gradually reduced their numbers, and after the Revolution, most of them went west to the territories in Canada." He shrugged. "I'm afraid life back home is not always as exciting as it is said to be."

"Oh, but, surely!" Sofia insisted. "I read somewhere only the other day that all Americans carry guns and that they often shoot at each other!"

He did not answer for a second or two. And Lucy, who had noticed the way in which his eyes had suddenly became the color of polished steel, was aware that, somehow, Sofia had crossed a line, that she had trodden, in her silly, tactless way, on forbidden territory. The next moment, he gave a rather grim smile.

"I find it rather surprising that people are willing to believe such nonsense," he said. "Perhaps in future, *signorina*, you should be a little more discriminating in your choice of reading material."

Sofia, not a bit put out, merely laughed at the barb, but Eduardo, sensing the sudden change in the atmosphere, got to his feet.

"Shall we go outside and enjoy the country air? I think it's time your charming cousin was given a tour of the grounds, don't you, Sofia?"

"It was ill-mannered of me to speak in that way to your cousin," Charles Ryman said, as they followed the others across the terrace. "I am sorry, and I will apologize to her."

"Sofia can sometimes be rather tactless," Lucy answered. "But she doesn't in the least mean to offend. It is just her way."

He nodded. "Surely."

"You see, America is so far away, and it seems to us such an exciting place."

"Indeed, it is. But I believe that most Europeans have rather an inaccurate view of life there. Generally speaking, we are quite a law-abiding nation."

"I suppose some people find the idea of lawlessness and guns thrilling," Lucy said. "Personally, I loathe violence of any kind. When I was a child, my father was brutally attacked and almost died. I have never forgotten the fear of losing him."

He glanced at her quickly. "That must have been very distressing."

"Yes. He means everything to me."

As they reached the shallow flight of steps leading to the gardens, he offered her his arm. "The grounds are extensive," he said. "And Eduardo likes to show them off. You mustn't let him tire you."

"Oh," she said, smiling, and her fingers trembled a little as she rested her hand on the fine broadcloth of his sleeve, "he will find it hard to do that. I have two young brothers at home, and I am used to keeping up with them when we go walking on the moors."

"May I ask where your home is?

"In Devonshire. Our house is on the edge of Dartmoor. Perhaps you have heard of it?"

He nodded. "Yes. I have spent some time in England, mainly in London. But I have friends there who have often spoken of the beauty of your countryside."

"Yes, it is beautiful, although some think it wild and uncivilized. But I love it, and I would never want to live anywhere else."

"Your family has roots there?"

"Yes," she said, proudly. "There have been Ashleighs at the Manor since the sixteenth century."

They walked on in silence for a while. Sofia and Eduardo were a considerable way ahead—no doubt a deliberate ploy on Sofia's part to leave Lucy alone with Major Ryman—but Lucy no longer cared. As hard as she tried to concentrate on the beauty of the extensive gardens, she was much more interested in the presence of the man at her side. It was a long time since she had enjoyed a walk so much.

"I hear," he said, as they paused near the rose garden to admire the ornate statuary at the fountain, "that you are to return home at the end of the month. Will you be sorry to leave Florence?"

"Yes, indeed. I have enjoyed my stay here very much. But I am looking forward to being with my family again."

"You have brothers, you say?" His eyes were alight with interest.

"Yes. Harry is almost ten years old, and Piers just eight. And my little sister, Antonia, recently had her sixth birthday."

She glanced up at him, watching him reflecting on the information. "My father was widowed soon after I was born," she added. "He married again when I was eleven."

Normally, Lucy found it hard to speak about her background, increasingly so of late because of the bitterness of her estrangement from James. But with Charles Ryman, her shyness seemed to leave her, and she was able to talk quite freely about her father and the love she had for him and for Adeline, her beloved stepmother. She told him how they had met when Adeline had come to teach the children of the poor in the village school and how, ten years on, they were still as much in love as ever.

"Your family means a great deal to you," he said, struck by the loving expression on her face as she talked of them.

"Yes. We are all very close."

She found herself telling him about her life in Lintern Magna, about the quiet country pleasures she enjoyed and the family and friends she valued. She described the sadness they had all felt when her great-uncle, Sir Roderick Ashleigh, had died after a fall from his horse. And how the whole village had turned out for the funeral of their beloved Squire in the parish church. She told him about her best friend, Grace Weston, and how she had been a bridesmaid at her wedding. And as she talked, she realized that the unhappiness that had clouded her life for the past months had slipped away almost without her noticing. And that somehow, although the man at her side knew nothing of what she had suffered, she was sure that if she had explained it to him, he would have understood.

It was only when he asked her how old her mother had been when she died that she remembered that, for most of the past hour, she had been confiding in a complete stranger and that it was probably time that she stopped.

"I'm so sorry," she said, rather breathlessly. "I'm afraid I have been talking about myself for far too long."

"No," he said. "Your conversation has given me more pleasure than I can say. I have enjoyed every moment of it. I envy you your family and the life you lead. It has made me realize how much I have missed by wandering about the world alone."

"But you have your home in New York?"

"I have a house in New York, yes," he said. "But I am rarely there. My parents are both dead, and I have no brothers or sisters. Three years ago, I left the Army and joined the Reserve to give me the freedom to take over the running of the family business. It was difficult at first, as I had much to learn. I had gone straight from West Point to join my regiment and knew nothing about antiques." He paused. "It was not a particularly happy time for me."

Lucy thought a shadow crossed his face as he spoke, and she glanced at him with a touch of curiosity. But the next moment, he had turned to her with a smile. "Most people would think that I am fortunate," he said. "And, of course, I am. Rymans imports antiques, and it is always a challenge to find interesting pieces. As a result, I travel a good deal, particularly in Europe."

"It must be fascinating!"

He shrugged. "My friends tell me," he said, "that it is high time I settled down and found some accommodating lady to marry." He tapped the toe of his riding boot with his walking stick and looked at her with a quizzical smile. "Tell me, what would your counsel be?"

Lucy was taken aback by the directness of the question. "I'm afraid I couldn't possibly comment," she said quickly. "I have no experience in these matters."

He turned to face her, the blue eyes taking hers prisoner. "So what I have been told is true. There really is no lovesick young man eagerly awaiting your return to Devonshire?"

The color rushed into her cheeks, and she gave him a swift, horrified glance. She had told no one but Sofia about James. Surely she had not betrayed her confidence by passing on the information to Eduardo? To her horror, she felt the hot pinpricks of tears behind her eyes as she suddenly pictured the amusement of the two men at her sad little story—and as she remembered how gaily she had chattered on about the joys of life at home. And all the time, Charles Ryman must have been laughing at her, knowing all along about the humiliation of the Wyatts' rejection of her as their prospective daughter-in-law.

"I'm sorry," he said quickly. "That was clumsy of me."

But she would not show him her distress. Her hand fell from his arm, and she turned away from him with her head held high.

"You are free to say what you wish, Major Ryman," she said, her voice low but controlled. "And now, if you will excuse me, I think that I would like to return to the house. I am feeling rather tired, and I have the beginnings of a headache."

Chapter Three

What a complete fool he had been! Charles stood on the terrace watching the landau disappearing down the drive on its way back to the Castello. He should have known better than to have spoken to Lucy Ashleigh so bluntly upon such a personal and intimate matter. He should have remembered that she was not what the Italians called a *donna di mondo*— a sophisticated woman of the world—but a gentle, unspoiled Englishwoman unused to the blasé manners of modern European society.

Eduardo had been completely nonplussed by the precipitate departure of the ladies, both of them obviously in a state of high agitation.

When he and Sofia had returned in excellent humor to the house, it was to find Charles alone in the loggia.

"Miss Ashleigh has gone indoors to rest," he had said in answer to Sofia's raised eyebrows. "She was feeling a little tired and was complaining of a headache."

And when, a short time later, the two ladies returned to join them, it was clear, to Eduardo's surprise and disappointment, that they were ready to leave.

Despite his protests and offers of further refreshment, he had no choice but to have the carriage brought 'round to take them home.

"I hope," Charles Ryman said to Sofia as the carriage was brought 'round, "you will forgive me if I appeared churlish earlier on." He glanced quickly at Lucy, who kept her eyes resolutely ahead. "It was uncalled for and most uncivil of me."

Sofia shook her head, laughing. "*Non e niente!* It's nothing!" And with a wave and a smile, they were gone.

"I'm afraid it was my fault that they left so soon. I think I upset Miss Ashleigh," Charles said. "I believe I asked too many personal questions."

Eduardo shook his head. "You Americans, you are too direct—how do you say it?—too blunt. You must be more careful what you say to young ladies, my friend, especially to the English. They are very correct, very formal."

"I was clumsy, I admit."

"What, exactly, did you say to Miss Ashleigh?"

"If you must know, I was trying to find out if, as you seemed to think, she really is unattached."

Eduardo's black eyes widened. "You are saying you are seriously interested in the young lady, my friend? She is, of course, most charming. But this is unlike you." He grinned mischievously. "Be careful, Charles! You might have your heart broken yet!"

The expression on the handsome face was suddenly remote. "Maybe," he said bleakly, "I have spent too long in Europe, and it is time I went home."

But later, when he was alone at the house he had taken near the Ponte Vecchio, he knew he had no intention of doing so, not just yet.

He had been instantly attracted to Lucy Ashleigh from the moment he had held her in his arms on the stairs at the Castello. Besides her beauty, there was a gravity and a sweetness about her that he found irresistible, and she was everything that he admired in a woman—intelligent, gentle, and refined. And yet, as he had found out today, to his cost, she had another side to her. She did not suffer fools gladly, and it would take more than the exchange of a few pleasantries to know her better.

Charles began to pace about the room restlessly. Today, before he had made a mistake and breached the strict code of English etiquette, he was certain that he had not imagined the mutual attraction between them. And yet, he told himself, he was more than ten years her senior, and they were worlds apart in terms of background and experience.

It would be, he thought, an act of selfishness on his part to try to engage her interest.

And yet, recalling those huge dark eyes that seemed to burn with life, and the sweet, smooth curve of her lips, he knew that he would not be able to walk away without seeing her again—whatever the consequences.

"I tell you, cousin, I said nothing to Eduardo! Nothing at all! I have no idea how Major Ryman came to know about James!"

Sofia's voice had been shrill with indignation when Lucy, on the journey home, repeated the question she had asked her earlier.

"But you were the only person I told here in Italy. At home, of course, it is common knowledge, but Mr. Ryman has never been anywhere near Lintern Magna."

"Then perhaps he has met someone from the county?"

"Impossible. He would have mentioned it."

Lucy stared ahead as the carriage sped through the darkening landscape. She wanted to believe her cousin, but she could see no explanation other than that Sofia had confided in Eduardo and was now reluctant to admit it.

"I beg you to believe me, *cara*!" Sofia laid a gloved hand on Lucy's arm. "I would never betray a confidence. You must have misunderstood what Major Ryman said."

Was that possible? Lucy tried to remember his exact words, but it was difficult to recall them precisely. She sighed. When all was said and done, what did it matter if her pride had been wounded? Her cousin had been a good friend to her during her stay at the Castello. She was not like her best friend, dear Grace, of course. Sofia was wayward and often capricious, but Lucy had no reason to doubt her word.

"You are probably right," she said. "Forgive me for doubting you!"

And there the matter ended. They began to talk about the beauty of the Villa San Matteo and of the hospitality they had received there. To Lucy's amusement, Sofia waxed lyrical on the subject of Eduardo while pretending not to be impressed by him. And by the time they reached the Castello, the tension between them had dissipated.

Even so, despite her efforts to be cheerful, Lucy went to her room feeling miserable and dejected. The day, which had begun with such promise, had been ruined for her. Sofia had made her realize that her sensitivity on the subject of James might have made her see offense where none had been intended. But it was of little comfort to remind herself that the remark Charles Ryman had made was of no significance—especially as she was never likely to meet him again.

The following morning, after breakfast, Sofia and Lucy were sitting together in the salon when Giovanni, the elderly major-domo, entered with a bouquet of white lilies and a letter on a silver tray.

Sofia put out her hand to take them from him, but he shook his head, his lined, rather melancholy face lit by a smile. Although she was his favorite, he had taken a fancy to the little English *signorina,* and he handed the flowers and the letter to her with a flourish.

"For me?" Her eyes widened in surprise as she put down her sketchbook to take them. She looked wonderingly at the exquisite blooms and picked up the square white envelope addressed to her in unfamiliar handwriting.

"*Presto!* Hurry!" Sofia, intrigued, urged her impatiently as Lucy drew out the single sheet of paper.

Dear Miss Ashleigh,

I beg you to forgive my rudeness yesterday. I should not have questioned you upon such a personal matter. I assure you, it was not my intention to give offense, and I hope you will accept my apology.

*I look forward to the possibility of meeting you again.
And remain,*

> *Respectfully yours,
> Charles Ryman*

Lucy's fingers trembled a little as she passed over the letter for her cousin to read. "You see?" Sofia said triumphantly. "It was all a misunderstanding! And," she added, clasping her hands in excitement, "I must tell you that in Italy, the lily is considered to be a token of admiration!" She gave a rapturous sigh. "I knew it! You were meant for each other!"

Lucy laughed rather unconvincingly. "Oh, really, Sofia? In England, the flower is merely a mark of respect, as it probably is in America."

But she suddenly felt lighter. Almost joyful, like a child who had been given a reprieve after some piece of bad behavior.

Charles Ryman had, she thought, very distinctive handwriting, the letters bold and well formed, without flourishes, and a clear, unadorned signature. It was courteous of him to write and apologize when he had probably not been at fault. And, yes, she thought tremulously, she, too, hoped that they would meet again.

Later, alone in her room, she put away the envelope in her writing case, and, as she did so, she was remembering the other letter that remained locked in her bureau at home When she returned home, she thought, she would destroy it.

After all, it belonged to the past.

Charles Ryman stared moodily out of the window of his carriage. The lights of the rivercraft lay like gold coins on the surface of the Arno, but tonight their beauty gave him no pleasure. All day, he had told himself that it was foolish of him to expect Miss Ashleigh to reply to his letter. What did he expect? They barely knew each other! But wherever he went, he lived in hope of some unexpected meeting with her, and it seemed to him that as each day passed, their brief and fragile connection was fast disappearing.

On arriving at the opera house, he joined a group of friends in their box some ten minutes before the curtain went up on Mozart's *The Magic Flute.* As he took his seat, he glanced casually around the crowded auditorium. And when some sixth sense had drawn his gaze to his left, he suddenly saw Lucy Ashleigh entering the box opposite his, with her cousin Sofia and her family.

The surge of excitement shooting through his veins at the sight of her sweet face was startling. It was, he told himself, utterly bizarre. He had only just made her acquaintance, and yet the desire to leave his seat and go immediately to her side was overwhelming.

She was wearing red—a simple but elegant gown with a heart-shaped neckline that enhanced the beauty of her coloring and left her creamy shoulders and arms bare. And, to his chagrin, she was deep in conversation with a handsome, olive-skinned young man who was obviously finding her company fascinating.

Riveted by the unexpected sight of her, he had to force himself to behave sociably and to concentrate on the conversation of the Baronessa di Stefano, the beautiful woman sitting at his side, who had invited him to join her party. She had made no secret of her interest in him since the moment they had met several weeks ago. And despite the fact that, after a number of carefully engineered meetings, Charles had remained quite clearly impervious to her charms, she continued to pursue him relentlessly.

"Charles? You do not seem yourself tonight." She placed her gloved hand on his arm possessively.

"Forgive me." He smiled. "I'm afraid I have a good deal on my mind."

"You men!" She leaned a little closer and tapped his shoulder with her fan flirtatiously. "Always worrying about business. You must learn to relax and enjoy the moment, *mio caro!*"

But when the lights dimmed, and the orchestra began the overture, Charles realized that any enjoyment of the evening's entertainment had been ruined for him. He sat, tense and preoccupied, unable to concentrate on the performance, aware of nothing but the fact that Lucy Ashleigh was sitting somewhere on his left in the darkness. And she would, he thought with a rueful smile, have absolutely no idea of his presence and not the slightest inkling of the effect she was having upon him.

In the first interval, people immediately began to move about and go in and out of the boxes. As Charles got to his feet and looked across, Lucy suddenly turned her head, and their eyes met in a long, lingering glance. He was rewarded by a smile of singular sweetness, and she raised a hand shyly in salute as he made her a bow. She had, he thought with a surge of relief, obviously forgiven him for his behavior at the Villa. Then, out of the corner of his eye, he saw Sofia waving at him and beckoning him to join them.

"Baronessa, would you please excuse me for a moment?" he murmured, and, ignoring her aggrieved glance, he made his way swiftly down the corridor to find the door of the box occupied by the di Lorenzo party standing ajar.

It was crowded, so full of laughing, chattering people, in fact, that it was impossible for him to get anywhere near Lucy. She was talking with the same young man who had claimed her attention earlier, her face upturned to his, and she gave no sign of having seen him enter. Achingly aware of her presence, of the curve of her cheek as she smiled, of the beauty of her slender figure, Charles found himself face-to-face with Eduardo Ortalli, who was delighted to see him, and he did his best to join in the general chatter. But his eyes returned again and again to Lucy, each time hoping for some sign that she was at least conscious of his nearness. And when she at last glanced in his direction, a small, regretful smile curved her lips, and he sensed the strange alchemy that somehow translated itself to them both without a word having been exchanged.

"I'm afraid, *mio amico*, that you are a doomed man," Eduardo said, laughing, following his line of sight. "But who can blame you? She is extremely alluring."

Charles threw him an impatient glance. He was in no mood

for Eduardo's sense of humor. He knew that he could not return to his seat without speaking to Lucy, and he was wondering exactly how he could intrude upon her conversation, when Sofia suddenly appeared at his elbow.

"Major Ryman! *Buona sera!* How pleasant to meet you once again."

He bowed. "*Signorina.* The pleasure is mine."

"I'm sure my cousin will also be delighted to see you." Smiling, she took his arm and led him, determinedly, through the crush of people. "Lucy! Look who is here!"

Lucy's hand in his, so small, so fragile, filled him with strange tenderness, and when he raised his eyes to hers, he was certain she let him hold it a fraction longer than was necessary.

But Sofia quickly claimed his attention. "Major Ryman, may I present my cousin Paolo Conti?"

The two men bowed, eyeing each other with faint hostility, but to Charles' relief, they had barely time to exchange the civilities before Sofia was wafting Paolo away.

"*Dio mio!* There is my friend Renata. Come, Paolo, I have promised to introduce you to her."

They stood, Charles and Lucy, face-to-face, surrounded by people but aware only of each other.

"Thank you so much for the flowers," she said, her dark eyes shy. "They were beautiful. But there was really no need to send them."

"Then you have forgiven me?"

"Of course. There is nothing to forgive."

"I very much enjoyed that day at the Villa San Matteo," he said. "And it's good to see you again. I never imagined that I would find you here tonight."

"Really?" She smiled. "I am fond of opera. But I have had so many social engagements lately that I almost decided not to come."

"I am very glad that you did. I was beginning to think that you might return to England before I had the chance to see you again."

She blushed, shaking her head.

"Are you enjoying the music?" she asked him, as if desperate to keep him at arm's length.

His eyes met hers, very level and direct. "I admire Mozart," he said. "But tonight I am finding it rather difficult to concentrate. My mind is elsewhere."

She glanced away quickly to cover her confusion.

"What a pity. It's such a fine performance."

Charles put out a hand to steady her as she was jostled by someone squeezing past, and he took her arm. The silky warmth of her shoulder under his fingers sent a shaft of desire through him.

"I was thinking," he said quickly, "that I would like to call on you at the Castello. Would that be at all possible?"

"I'm not certain." She made an odd little gesture, conveying her sudden confusion. "My great-grandmother insists on a rather strict code of etiquette. And as I am a guest in her house . . ."

"Of course," he said gravely. "I wouldn't dream of breaking the rules."

And then, as the bell sounded, ending the interval, he bent over her hand.

"*À bientôt*, then," he said, and he turned to make his way through the throng to rejoin his party.

"Charles! At last! We thought you had deserted us," the Baronessa whispered as he took his seat just as the lights dimmed.

She had clearly been put out by his absence and was even more disappointed when he declined her invitation to join her for a late supper with the rest of the party, but Charles was too preoccupied to care. He spent the rest of the evening reliving his brief exchange with Lucy and telling himself he had not imagined the magnetism between them. True, she had refused his request to call, but something told him that, although she was trying to observe the proprieties, he would not be unwelcome.

But later, as he walked home alone through the dark streets, his feeling of excitement and euphoria drained away from him, and he cursed himself for his foolishness. The past suddenly bore down on him, crushing his hopes. Whatever lay between him and Lucy Ashleigh, he told himself, should best be left undisturbed. And yet, while reason assured him of its wisdom, his heart was telling him a very different story.

Chapter Four

Lucy had no idea exactly how and when she had become separated from Sofia as they wandered in the Piazza Signoria the following day.

They had set out from the Castello early with the intention of finding suitable souvenirs for Lucy to take home with her, and she had looked forward to the outing. Her stepmother collected Murano glass, and Sofia knew where she might be able to purchase an antique vase that would please Adeline. On the last occasion on which she and Sofia had been there, they had been obliged to cut short their visit because of a sudden thunderstorm.

As they emerged from the loggia and slowly threaded their way through the throngs of sightseers, Lucy stopped briefly to look at an equestrian statue. The rider's patrician Roman features were strangely reminiscent of another face she admired, and she stared at it in fascination.

She had not been able to stop thinking about Charles Ryman since the night at the opera. She had seen him enter and had been shocked by the surge of jealousy she had felt as she watched him in conversation with the beautiful woman sitting next to him. She remembered every small detail of the scene. Charles, so handsome and elegant in evening dress, his fair head bent solicitously toward his companion. Her jeweled hand on his arm, the little, flirtatious flick of the ivory-and-lace fan that seemed to hint at an intimacy with each other.

She had been unable to resist asking Paolo, who sat next to her, who the lady was.

"That is the Baronessa di Stefano, one of the richest women

in Florence," he explained. "Her husband died some years ago and left her a huge fortune."

Lucy's heart had plummeted. Not only beautiful but wealthy as well!

But what did she expect? Everyone said Major Ryman was a philanderer. And yet, he had left the Baronessa's side and come to her in the interval. The memory of that thrillingly intense look in his eyes as he said her name, of the touch of his hand on her shoulder, of their brief but deeply intimate conversation filled her with excitement.

But she blushed to remember how clumsily she had dealt with his request to call. It was because she knew that the Contessa disapproved of Charles Ryman, and she was afraid of incurring her displeasure.

Charles Ryman had become a guilty secret she was unable to share even with Sofia. It must be, she told herself, merely infatuation. She had never felt like this about James, she thought, never trembled when he looked at her as Charles had done the other night, never longed to be alone with him, never dreamed of . . . Heavens! Blushing at the wickedness of her thoughts, she tore her eyes away from the statue. And it was when she turned to glance over her shoulder that she realized, with a stab of alarm, that she had lost sight of Sofia.

Anxiously, she looked from left to right, hoping for a glimpse of her cousin's feathered hat and bright blue gown, but there was no sign of her. She seemed to have vanished into thin air. Minutes slipped by as Lucy gazed around the sunlit square, wondering if she should remain where she was or retrace her steps. She stared up at the tall, crenellated tower of the Palazzo. At half past eleven on an August morning, the sun was beating down pitilessly upon the crowded piazza, and, despite her parasol, she felt almost dizzy with the heat.

Where on earth could Sofia be? Perhaps, Lucy thought, as a noisy group of sightseers pushed past, calling out to one another in loud foreign voices, she should try to make her way to the place where Guido, their groom, was waiting with the carriage. She could ask him to go in search of her cousin.

Yet, on the other hand, if she stayed where she was, perhaps Sofia would return to find her. She hesitated. Standing there alone, dressed as she was in white muslin trimmed with satin ribbons and carrying an embroidered parasol in the same deep shade of pink, she was beginning to attract attention, particularly from the daring young Italian males promenading in the piazza.

Feeling distinctly nervous, she turned to walk toward the loggia, felt a hand pluck at her sleeve, and whirled around to find herself surrounded by half a dozen dirty, ragged urchins clamoring for lire.

"*Per favore, signorina, per favore!*"

They plucked at her gown with filthy, clawlike hands, pressing closer and closer, and Lucy, in sudden panic, dropped her parasol as she reached for her purse.

As she fumbled for money, the noisy gang suddenly ceased their impudent demands and fell back as a tall figure appeared at Lucy's side and threatened them with his cane.

"*Vada via!*" Charles Ryman flung a handful of coins at them, and as they scrambled for them in the dirt, he retrieved the parasol and led Lucy away.

Almost dizzy with fright, she clung to his arm. "Thank you," she murmured, as he led her toward the fountain. "Thank you so much."

He stared down at her, frowning. "What in heaven's name are you doing here alone?" he asked her sternly. "Don't you realize how dangerous it is?"

She freed her arm and forced herself to look up at him. "Sofia and I were together until a few minutes ago. We became separated somehow," she said defensively. "I was about to go back to the loggia to see if I could find her."

"That would be pointless. It would be far too crowded," he said, his curt tone disguising his concern for her. "There are some small tables under an awning near the center of the square where they offer refreshment. I believe it is a well-known meeting place." He offered her his arm. "You had better come and wait there with me."

And Lucy, almost tearful after her fright, was only too happy to do as he asked.

"Let me order you something cold to drink," Charles said, as she sank down gratefully at a table in the shade. "A glass of *limoncello*? Some cordial? Or water, perhaps?"

"Thank you, no." Lucy's throat was parched, but Sofia had warned her not to drink water in Italy unless she was sure it had been boiled. She had no idea what American ladies drank in public, but anything stronger for her was quite out of the question.

She forced a smile. "It seems that I am once again indebted to you, Major Ryman. This is the second time you have been obliged to come to my rescue."

"It was entirely my pleasure. But I would counsel you to take care when you visit places like this. The incident today was bad enough, but you might easily have suffered a worse fate. These crowded squares are alive with thieves and pickpockets."

"I'm sure you're right." Lucy, recovering from her fright, found herself struggling to sound calm and self-assured. "I was just about to say how fortuitous it is that you happened to be here this morning."

"Not really," he said. "You see, I called at the Castello earlier to leave my card, and I was told I might find you here."

Lucy stared at him in disbelief. "You came here to find me?"

"Yes." He looked at her across the table, his gaze very candid and direct. "It was impossible to talk last night, and I wanted to make sure you really had forgiven me for upsetting you the other afternoon."

Her cheeks flamed as she remembered how she had stormed off into the villa. "It was nothing," she murmured. "Just a misunderstanding on my part. And you were right. There is no one, as you put it, eagerly awaiting my return to England. You see, I thought, quite wrongly, that you were referring to something that happened to me some months ago."

He raised a sardonic eyebrow. "Now I am even more confused."

Lucy raised her eyes to his. Suddenly she did not care if Charles Ryman, or anyone else, for that matter, knew about James. It was all rather distant and unimportant, almost as if it had happened a long time ago to someone else.

"It's really quite simple," she said, and her lovely eyes were candid as they met his. "Someone once asked me to marry him, and I said I would. But then he changed his mind. I thought that perhaps someone had told you about it."

He stared at her in consternation. "I had absolutely no idea. And even if I had known, believe me, I would never have referred to it."

"Of course not. It was foolish of me to think such a thing. And in any case, it is time I put it all behind me."

"Easier said than done." He smiled, rather bleakly. "There was someone in my life once who . . ." He stopped. "But that," he said quickly, "was a long time ago. We were talking about you."

He reached out and laid his hand on her arm—a brief, unexpected, and completely indecorous gesture, which turned her heart over. "Unless, of course, you'd rather not?"

"No, I wish to, but there really isn't much to tell. His parents objected to the match. They did not think it . . . I was suitable."

"Not suitable?" The blue eyes widened in disbelief. "I don't understand."

"It was my background. It is rather . . . unconventional. And James' father would have disowned him if he had married me."

There was a long silence. "He allowed that to come between you?" he said at last, his voice filled with contempt.

"He had no choice."

He looked at her fiercely. "The man is nothing but a fool and a coward."

"No," she said quickly. "James is neither. We have known each other since we were children, and he would never willingly have done anything to hurt me. But, you see, his father is an earl, and I should have realized that I would not be considered acceptable."

"Forgive me if I appear ignorant," he said. "I'm afraid the English class system has always been a mystery to me. In what possible way could a lady like yourself be thought unsuitable?"

Lucy met his glance. She was not used to such directness, but she was finding it undeniably refreshing to be able to talk so freely. Suddenly, she felt sure that she could tell Charles Ryman anything without being judged or condemned.

"It is really quite simple," she said again. "You see, when my father was seventeen, he fell in love with a servant—one of the maids who worked at the Manor. She was my mother."

Charles' expression did not change. He merely waited for her to go on with her story.

"Naturally, his uncle, Sir Roderick, who was his guardian, was furious and sent him abroad. In fact, he came here to Florence to study. But he had married my mother in secret before he left, and while he was away, my mother gave birth to me. She had no way of letting him know that he had a child, and she died in poverty a few weeks later. I was brought up in a workhouse, and I was ten years old before my father at last found me and took me home."

"That is an amazing and wonderful story."

She smiled. "I have an amazing and wonderful family. My stepmother was instrumental in rescuing me and uniting me with my father. I love them both dearly. But now, perhaps, you can understand why it would be impossible for the son of an earl to marry the daughter of a parlor maid."

"No," he said, "I'm afraid I do not."

"But don't you see? James would have lost everything."

"Except what was most precious," he said quietly. "You."

The blue eyes flashed a message to her, one that was quite clear and explicit. There was a sense of being carried inexorably into deep water. And although the current of emotion threatened to overwhelm her, Lucy had no desire to struggle against it.

There was no knowing where the conversation would have led had Sofia not chosen that precise moment to appear. She flew at her cousin in an ecstasy of relief.

"Lucy!" Flushed and agitated, she almost overturned the table. "*Dio mio!* Where have you been? I stopped only for a moment to greet a friend, and you had vanished! Guido is waiting with the carriage, and I was about to—" Then, suddenly aware of the man at Lucy's side, she stopped abruptly in midflow. "Major Ryman! *Per favore*, please excuse my rudeness. I have been so worried about my cousin!"

Already on his feet, he removed his hat and bowed. "*Signorina.*"

"Some beggars came up to me demanding money," Lucy said quickly, feeling the need to explain. "I'm afraid I became rather panic-stricken and dropped my parasol, and Major Ryman kindly came to the rescue."

Sofia burst out laughing. "*Mille grazie*, Major!" She threw her hands in the air. "I'm afraid that my cousin simply cannot be trusted out of my sight!"

"It was my pleasure." He was looking at Lucy in a way that excluded the entire world.

"We really must go." Sofia, who had noted the glance, took her cousin's arm firmly. "We are lunching with Great-Grandmother, and we dare not be late."

Charles nodded and offered them an arm each. "Then please allow me to escort you ladies to your carriage."

As they made their way across the piazza, Sofia turned to him. "How did you enjoy the opera the other night? I thought Adelina Patti was magnificent! And she is so beautiful, don't you agree?"

"I'm afraid," he said, glancing at Lucy, "I was distracted. My mind was elsewhere that evening."

"You should have stayed with us in our box after the interval. I should like to have introduced you to my brothers," Sofia said artlessly. She glanced up at him speculatively. "I have just remembered that we are all going to Fiesole for a picnic on Thursday. Perhaps you would like to join the family party?

Eduardo has promised to come, and we would enjoy your company, would we not, Lucy?"

Lucy nodded, not quite daring to meet his eyes. "Of course."

"That is kind of you. But I would not wish to intrude."

"Nonsense! You would be most welcome. In fact," Sofia said, with a mischievous smile, "I must insist that you come. You must be on hand in case my cousin once again needs rescuing!"

Lucy was still blushing when they set off back to the Castello. But when she tried to remonstrate with her cousin about her shamefully unsubtle attempts to throw her and Major Ryman together, Sofia refused to listen.

"As if I needed to!" she said scornfully. "It is perfectly obvious that he is in love with you. And please don't try to pretend that you do not like him, *cara*. I see it in your eyes every time you look in his direction!"

Lucy reddened. She could barely bring herself to admit to herself how Charles Ryman made her feel, let alone confess such a thing to her cousin. No man had ever produced such an effect upon her. Certainly, she realized, in wonder, not James! What she had felt for him had been great affection, a warmth that sprang from their easy familiarity and friendship. She had never before felt this tumult of excitement, this sweet, bewildering sensation spreading through her whenever she was near Charles Ryman

She tried to tell herself that this was only a natural reaction to the romance and magic of Italy, that when she returned home, the whole foolishness would end. She would forget and pick up the threads of her life and go on as if she had never met him.

But two days later, the touch of his hand as he helped her into the carriage that was to take them to Fiesole filled her with the same breathless excitement, and she made no attempt to resist it.

The breezy hilltops above Florence had always been one of the di Lorenzos' favorite retreats from the summer heat of the city. They had needed three carriages to convey the entire party and the provisions for a picnic on the brief excursion. Sofia's three brothers sat up on the boxes with the grooms. Their wives joined Sofia in the leading carriage with Eduardo, while the second carriage overflowed with the younger Lorenzo children and their nannies. Charles had then followed Lucy, as if it was the most natural thing in the world, into the third carriage, and they sat side by side opposite Sofia's two young nephews.

As they climbed high above the city, Lucy sat very still, her hands folded in her lap, and tried to concentrate on the beauty of the surrounding countryside. Impossible, she thought, with Charles' sleeve brushing her arm and with the solemn gaze of the two little boys sitting opposite.

"My father say you are *soldato*. That you fight in the American war," the elder of the two said, his brown eyes examining Charles eagerly.

"That's true."

"You have a sword?"

"I have."

"And you will show it to us?" his brother asked earnestly.

"Someday, perhaps."

Satisfied with his reply, they seemed content to spend the rest of the journey in respectful contemplation of their distinguished traveling companion and asked no further questions.

It was a strangely peaceful journey. Charles had said little to Lucy after greeting her—the merest of polite inquiries about her health—but the quality of the silence between them had a strange, exclusive intimacy. And she was content to sit there at his side, so close that she could catch the sharp, clean scent of his cologne and feel the warm pressure of his arm against hers as the jolting of the wheels over the uneven ground threw them together.

Too soon they arrived at the deserted piazza in Fiesole and were obliged to leave the carriages to take the narrow path to the grassy plateau where the picnic would take place.

Perhaps, Lucy thought nervously, it was no accident that she found herself walking with Charles at some distance behind the rest of the party. The two little boys had run off with wild shouts of excitement the minute the carriage had come to a halt, and it seemed to her that Charles had deliberately slowed their pace as they followed the others.

The air was much cooler here, she noticed, and a light breeze fluttered the skirt of her gown and ruffled the tendrils of dark hair escaping from her bonnet.

"Would you like to go inside the cathedral?" Charles asked her as they approached the Duomo of San Romolo.

Lucy looked up at the bell tower high above the gray limestone walls and hesitated. She had noticed, with a little stab of guilt, that the rest of the party had passed by the entrance and had disappeared from sight. But suddenly, the desire to be alone with Charles Ryman seemed to override her normal awareness of decorum. "Yes," she said, boldly. "I should like to. It might be interesting."

They entered the church together, blinded for a few moments by the contrast between the dazzling sunlight outside and the cold dimness of the interior. The scent of incense hung in the air, and Lucy followed her companion up the nave toward the high altar, gazing, fascinated, at the sculptures and the frescoes adorning the stone walls. Their footsteps echoed in the silence. They stood for a while looking up at the exquisite altarpiece that depicted the Virgin and Child and, above them, the roof of bright blue studded with stars. And then Charles left her side, went into a little side chapel, and lit a candle.

He stood perfectly still for a few seconds with his head bowed. Lucy could not see his face in the dim gray light, but there was a strange humility in his manner that she found very moving. Then he raised his head and, without a word, led the way to the west door.

Struck by the gesture he had made, she glanced at him curiously. She longed to know why and for whom he had lit the candle. It was, she thought, obviously someone he cared about very deeply. But she did not feel she could ask.

Unaccountably, she shivered as they emerged into the hot sunshine, and he looked at her sharply.

"I hope you haven't had too much sun." He took her parasol and put it up for her.

"No," she said. "There is always something about the atmosphere in these places that affects me. There is such a sense of antiquity—something that makes me feel utterly insignificant."

"You could never be insignificant," he said, and something about his tone made her tremble.

"We had better try to catch up with the others," she said hastily.

"Unfortunately, I suppose we must."

She looked at him, startled and a little hurt.

"I thought you wished to join our family excursion."

"Oh, I did," he said, as they turned into the Via San Francesco, "and it was good of your cousin to invite me. But I came because I wanted to be with you."

Lucy felt the quick color rushing into her face. She had no idea what to say. She knew nothing of dalliances and could only blurt out the first thing that came into her head.

"How kind of you to say so."

"Kind?" He stopped and turned to look at her. "It's not kind at all," he said, almost angrily. "It happens to be the truth. From the moment I saw you at the Castello, I have thought about you constantly. Forgive me for speaking so bluntly. I don't know how else to explain how very much I admire you."

Lucy caught her breath, staring at him with shocked, startled eyes, and her hand went to her lips with a quick, involuntary gesture.

If she had been a little older, if she had not led such a sheltered life in the quiet English backwater of Devonshire, she might have been able to deal with the situation. As it was, the bluntness of Charles Ryman's approach filled her with utter confusion. This was not, in her limited knowledge of the etiquette of courtship, how a gentleman should speak to a lady. And her own bewildering feelings toward him made her predicament seem even more alarming.

"Forgive me," he said, "if, once again, I have spoken out of turn. Have I offended you?"

Lucy stood very still, her gaze held by his. She stared up into his brilliant eyes, and it was as if he had cast a spell, making her incapable of movement or speech.

Then, quite suddenly, she found her voice. "No," she whispered. "I am not offended."

He took her hand, then, in his. "This morning, when I woke," he said, "all I could think about was that soon I would be seeing you. And I realized that I have never, in all my life, felt that way about anyone else."

It was a moment she knew she would never forget.

They stood motionless, gazing into each other's eyes, and when he pressed her hand to his lips, Lucy knew that something precious and lovely had entered her life.

It was she who first became sane, glancing over her shoulder in a panic at the sound of voices close by. They moved apart just before the two small boys who had been sent to find them appeared at the end of the path, waving and calling to them.

"Please wait," he said urgently, as, hot and flustered, she turned quickly to walk on. "Don't run away. I leave for Rome at the end of the week. May I see you before I go? Tomorrow maybe?"

"It's not possible," she said, her voice unsteady. The sight of the two boys had brought her back to earth with a crash, and she quickened her pace. "Sofia has arranged to go to Valdarno tomorrow to visit a friend."

"But it is not your cousin I want to see," he said dryly, his mouth crinkling at the corners.

Still trembling, she shook her head. "You know I cannot be alone with you without a chaperone."

"And I also know," he said, "that I cannot leave Florence until I have seen you again. I shall be at the Rose Garden below the Piazza Michelangelo at three o'clock tomorrow afternoon. I will wait for you near the Fountain of Venus. Will you come?"

The sound of voices and laughter close by meant that soon they would catch up with the others, and Lucy knew she must give him an answer.

"I will try," she whispered at last.

It was dangerous and foolish, and she would probably live to regret it, but at that moment, as she walked in the sunshine with Charles Ryman at her side, she really did not care.

Lucy was desperate to avoid Sofia's curious eyes as she and Charles joined the others.

"There you are!" Her cousin gave her a long, searching glance. "Did you find the church interesting?"

"Very," she said, looking away quickly. "Heavens, this looks wonderful! What a treat!"

The picnic had been arranged on a grassy plateau that provided breathtaking views of the city below. Lucy had not been prepared for such an elaborate occasion or such a vast array of food. Her only experience of picnics was of those she had enjoyed with the family at home, informal affairs in the Manor woods and fields that were often shared with friends and sometimes included the servants. But here, they were seated, each member of the party, on special cushions around a snow-white cloth and were waited upon by grooms who had been especially chosen for the task.

Lucy sat down, with downcast eyes, opposite Charles and tried to smile and behave normally. She found it impossible to look in his direction, but she was acutely aware of him with every fiber of her being. And she knew that he, too, felt the same powerful magnetism that had drawn them inexorably together.

Somehow, she forced herself to laugh and talk and to give every sign of enjoying herself. Was it her imagination, or was Eduardo looking at her curiously? And why were Sofia's sisters-in-law staring at Charles Ryman and whispering behind their fans?

The air rang with the sound of their voices as they chattered and argued happily together. Their plump, gorgeous babies rolled about on the grass with their nannies, and the older children squabbled over their toys and chased one another across the meadow.

Lucy had become used to their noisy, joyful family gatherings, but they all spoke so quickly that, although her Italian was now more fluent, she did not feel confident enough to make much of a contribution to the general conversation.

Charles seemed perfectly relaxed as he discussed the possibility of a hunting trip later on in the year with Eduardo and the other men. But each time she risked a glance in his direction, she found his eyes on her face, inviting her to join him in an intimate conspiracy. And somehow, despite her surroundings, she found it more and more difficult to tear her eyes away. Already she had begun to think of a way in which she could go alone to the Rose Garden to meet him, and the mere thought of it filled her with a kind of fearful excitement.

When at last they had finished eating, Eduardo suggested a walk to the ancient Roman amphitheater.

"Come, Charles," he said, taking his friend's arm. "This will fascinate you. It was built in the first century B.C. and can hold three thousand spectators." He turned and looked at the others. "Will anyone else join us?"

The rest of the party, who had already viewed the tiers of stone seats on other occasions, declined, but Sofia, who wished to speak to Lucy alone, insisted that they follow the two men.

"Tell me at once! What has happened between you and Major Ryman?" she demanded as soon as they were out of earshot of the others. "Why were you so long at the Duomo?"

Lucy kept her eyes firmly on the ground. "We . . . I thought it very impressive. It really is quite beautiful, and the frescoes are exquisite."

Sofia gave her cousin's arm a little shake. "Do you think I am blind? I saw your face when you joined us. What has he said to you?"

Lucy shook her head. She knew she could not possibly tell her cousin what had really transpired. "It was nothing, I promise you. He merely said that he . . ." Her voice faltered. ". . . he admired me."

Sofia gave a gasp, and her black eyes shone with excitement. "I knew it! Did I not tell you he was in love with you, *cara*?

Those blue eyes! They say so much when he looks at you. And you—you don't deny that you feel something for him, do you?"

"I am flattered by his interest," Lucy said rather desperately. "I did not expect to receive such a compliment."

Sofia laughed scornfully. "My dearest Lucy! So English! So proper and so correct! But do not forget that you also have warm Italian blood running through your veins. You cannot deny that."

And Lucy, with her eyes on the tall, fair-haired figure walking ahead, knew in her heart that her cousin was quite right. For a moment, she was tempted to tell Sofia that she had decided to accept Charles Ryman's invitation to walk with her in the Rose Garden the following afternoon. But only for a moment. It would not be fair to involve Sofia in her plan. If the Contessa found out that she had deliberately flouted the rules of etiquette, they would both be in serious trouble.

This was something she must keep to herself, she thought, firmly changing the subject, and when they joined the two men at the amphitheater, she was careful not to look in Charles Ryman's direction.

Even so, standing there with him, deeply conscious of his presence, of even the smallest movement he made, she found it difficult to concentrate as Eduardo extolled the beauty surrounding them, pointing out the ruins of a Roman theater and baths. When Charles turned to help her as she stumbled a little over the rough ground, the muscular strength of his forearm under her fingers sent the blood tingling through her veins. *Here I am,* she thought bemusedly, *in one of the most historic sites in Tuscany, and all I can think about is the set of a man's broad shoulders, the brilliance of his eyes, and the warmth of the smile meant for me and me alone.*

Taken all in all, she thought as they retraced their steps to join the others, it had been a memorable day. But the journey home was an anticlimax. Eduardo, having announced that he was tired of listening to the ladies' conversation, insisted that Lucy should join Sofia and took her place in the third carriage. By the time they arrived back at the Castello, her earlier euphoria was dissipating, and she was beginning to have serious misgivings about her plans for the following day. The mere thought of what her father would think of her behavior filled her with trepidation.

But as Charles Ryman took his leave of her and bowed over her hand, he looked up into her eyes with a glance that said everything.

"Until tomorrow." His lips silently formed the words. And in that moment, before she followed the others into the Castello, Lucy knew that she was entirely lost.

Chapter Five

A headache?" Sofia, with her head cocked to one side, regarded her cousin critically. "*E vero?* Perhaps I will ask Great-Grandmother to give you some laudanum."

"No, really, there is no need. It is merely because I slept so badly last night. I shall just stay quietly in my room until I feel better. Please don't concern yourself about me. Go and enjoy your visit to Valdarno."

Sofia had been surprised and disappointed when Lucy announced that she had decided not to accompany her. They had planned to stay overnight at the family home of her friend Olivia, and she had been looking forward to the visit.

Her dark eyes had been skeptical when Lucy had pleaded weariness and a headache. But it was perfectly true. She had hardly slept a wink all night, and her head had been throbbing from tension and weariness from the moment she had opened her eyes the following day.

The mere thought of her clandestine meeting with Charles Ryman filled her with delicious terror. But there was never a doubt about her decision. The desire to see him again outweighed every other consideration, but her heart beat fast at the thought of her own audacity.

After Sofia had left later that morning, the Contessa had sent her own personal maid to her with chamomile tea—her special cure for headaches and nervous exhaustion—and she had been given strict instructions to rest quietly in her room for the rest of the day.

Lucy had sipped the tea and had tried to lie down in the dimness of her shuttered room, but it was impossible to relax.

She sent back the tray the maid brought her at midday—she was far too nervous to eat—and found herself pacing about in her room while she waited for the rest of the household to take their siesta so that she could slip away from the Castello unseen.

She knew she had never in all her life contemplated doing anything quite as daring, and as she dressed, her anxiety steadily increased. She wanted to look her best, but she knew she should not wear anything that might draw attention. Dress after dress was discarded as she changed her mind a dozen times. In the end, hot and flustered with nerves and exertion, she settled upon a silk dress of silver gray with puffed sleeves and a small bustle. Trimmed with lace, the square-necked bodice was finished with tiny buttons made of mother-of-pearl. Her fingers shook as she fastened them. What would her parents think if they knew of her plans? What if she was somehow prevented at the last minute from escaping the watchful eye of the Contessa? And, even more disturbing, what if Charles Ryman had changed his mind?

When at last she was ready to leave her room, she went to stand before the mirror. The face staring back at her was flushed, her eyes huge with excitement and trepidation. What on earth did she think she was doing? She knew that it was inviting disaster to venture out alone in a city like Florence. That distressing incident with the beggar children had taught her that. But with that thought came the image of Charles Ryman waiting for her in the Rose Garden, and she knew there was no turning back.

With her heart in her mouth, Lucy tiptoed down the flight of stone stairs that led to the servants' quarters and slipped through a side entrance into the sun-baked street. To her relief, it was reassuringly empty, the city asleep during the siesta. Already, a new fear had entered her mind. It was past three o'clock, much later than she had intended to set out. With every moment that passed, she became more and more convinced that when she arrived at the garden, Major Ryman might have given up hope of seeing her and left. By the time she had reached the entrance to the Giardino delle Rose, some tiny, frightened part of her began to wish that her fears would be confirmed.

It was a fleeting thought, swept away by a surge of excitement when a tall figure in an elegant gray frock coat came striding toward her, his handsome face alight with relief and pleasure.

"Miss Ashleigh!" He bowed over her hand. "I was beginning to think you had changed your mind."

"I'm sorry," Lucy, praying that she did not look as flustered as she felt, said nervously. "I couldn't leave . . . it was difficult . . . I didn't mean to keep you waiting."

"You are here now." The warmth of his smile embraced her. "That is all that matters."

As they took the path toward the fountain, he offered her his arm. And as she walked with him, with her hand in the crook of his elbow, her initial nervousness began, miraculously, to vanish. She looked around her with a sigh of pleasure. She had never seen such a vast collection of roses or such a profusion of colors and scents.

"This is all so beautiful."

"Yes," he said. "Beautiful." But he was looking at her.

Near the fountain, he led her out of the sun to a rustic bench under the shade of a cypress tree.

"Shall we sit down?"

To be so near him made Lucy a little breathless. *I shall always remember this moment*, she thought. The roses, red and pink and white, casting their fragrance all around them, the white pathway strewn with fallen petals, and the afternoon sun glittering through the trembling leaves—all of it imprinted itself on her memory.

She was so close to him that she could see the tiny pulse beating fast under the smooth skin just beneath his ear, and there were flecks of silver in the blue of his eyes. The handsome features looked stern, she thought, but there was tenderness in the firm mouth. And then she was suddenly forced to avert her eyes in case he read her thoughts, which at that moment were quite improper.

"I hope," he said, misreading the expression on her face, "that your cousin was not too put out by having to go to Valdarno without you."

Lucy gave a conscience-stricken little smile. "Sofia was rather disappointed. She had been looking forward to introducing me to her friend. But I'm sure she will enjoy herself. And there will be other opportunities to meet Olivia before I leave."

He glanced at her quickly. "And when will that be?"

"Not for a few more weeks. I shall be home in time for my father's birthday." She smiled. "In fact, I have already found a gift for him. Sofia took me to a wonderful glove maker who has made him a pair of leather gauntlets. I know he will love to wear them this winter when he hunts."

"Do you hunt with him?"

"Occasionally. Although I hate seeing an animal killed. But I love riding. I didn't learn until I was ten years old, so I am not as accomplished as my brothers. They were put astride their ponies when they were tiny boys." She glanced at him, conscious that she was talking too much about herself. "I expect it was the same for you."

He smiled. "I think I was destined to be a cavalryman from birth."

"Really? My father would find that fascinating."

"Do you?"

Blushing deeply, she gave him a quick, sideways glance. "Of course."

"But not, I suspect, as fascinating as I find you."

She looked away, shocked, yet inside, she felt a thrill of delight.

"Forgive me," he said quickly. "Once again, I'm afraid I'm too blunt."

She smiled. "Perhaps it is because Americans are more outspoken than the English."

"Or maybe it is because the English are too reserved for their own good."

Her laugh was forced. "But there are times, surely, when it is best to keep one's feelings to oneself."

"True. But occasionally, two people can find a natural rapport between them and can trust each other enough to be honest and open." His eyes lingered on hers. "The other day, at the piazza, you felt able to tell me about the romance that ended so painfully for you."

"Yes, I did."

"Then may I ask if you still have feelings for the young man?"

Again, his forthright manner was disconcerting. "No," she said. "I shall always be fond of James, but I know now that we would not have made each other happy." She gave a faint smile. "Is that open enough for you?"

"Yes." He looked at her and smiled. "You see, I wanted to be sure how you felt before I spoke to you about my own feelings."

Lucy's face went hot, and she made a quick, defensive gesture. "Major Ryman . . ."

"Please, call me Charles."

She shook her head in confusion. "I don't think that would be appropriate. We scarcely know each other."

"That's true." His eyes were clear and blue as they gazed into hers "But you see," he said, "I feel as if I have been waiting to know you all my life."

Lucy looked at him, spellbound. The intensity of his tone made her heart beat so loudly that she was afraid he might be able to hear it.

"Please don't say any more." Suddenly the shocking impropriety of the situation dawned on her. Not only had she defied the rules her great-grandmother had laid down for her by going out in public, unchaperoned, with a man she barely knew. But she had actually allowed him to take advantage of the situation and speak to her in this utterly inappropriate manner!

"I shouldn't be here alone with you," she murmured distractedly. "You know that."

"Yes. But I am going to Rome at the end of the week, and I could not endure the thought of returning and finding you gone."

She shook her head. "I told you, I shall be here until the end of the month." She gave a tremulous little smile. "So I am sure we will meet again."

"And do you want that?"

"Yes." She looked at his mouth and saw that there was passion there as well as tenderness. She knew that he was going to kiss her, and when he bent his head, she raised her mouth to his. A flame leaped up inside her as their lips met and sent the blood racing through her veins, and for a few heady moments, she lost awareness of her surroundings. She was trembling when he raised his head, her lips parted, her eyes like stars.

"Lucy"—he caught her hands in his—"I think I have been in love with you since the moment we met. And just then, you made me believe you returned my feelings."

Lucy was trying very hard to compose herself. The hot color that had surged into her cheeks had receded, leaving her pale. Of course she was in love with him! She had known that all along, and suddenly she no longer cared that she had just given herself away. She opened her mouth to speak, and then, quite suddenly, the spell was broken.

A man's shadow abruptly blocked out the sun, and the figure standing there brought them both, with guilty haste, to their feet.

"Charles! Miss Ashleigh! *Buon giorno!*" said Eduardo Ortalli, with a sweeping bow.

Afterward, Lucy could barely remember stumbling through the awkward pleasantries, hideously aware of the compromising situation she had found herself in. But after the initial shock of the sudden encounter, Charles seemed perfectly at ease, quite unrepentant, and almost defiant.

"What brings you here, my friend?" he asked calmly.

"I am going to an exhibition of Roman artifacts at the Bardini Gallery nearby and decided to take the path through the rose gardens." Eduardo's black eyes examined them with undisguised curiosity. "Perhaps you would both like to join me? They say that some of the exhibits are fascinating."

"Thank you," Lucy said, her voice not quite steady. "But it

is time I returned to the Castello. My great-grandmother will be expecting me."

Charles nodded. "And I must go too. I have an important evening appointment."

"A pity!" Eduardo shrugged, carefully casual. "Please give my respects to the Contessa, Miss Ashleigh. And, of course, to my dear cousin Sofia." And then, as if he could no longer resist a gibe, he added, "I am surprised that she did not wish to join you on such a beautiful afternoon."

"Sofia has gone to visit a friend in Valdarno." Lucy raised her eyes to his, and although her cheeks were flushed, she held his gaze defiantly. "But I shall certainly pass on your regards to her when she returns tomorrow."

Eduardo bowed. *"Molto grazie."* He turned to Charles. "Shall we be seeing you at the Baronessa's birthday celebrations on Saturday, *mio amico*? I'm told it is to be a fabulous occasion."

"I'm afraid not. I have already made my apologies, as I am leaving for Rome the day before."

"Of course. I had forgotten."

Before he took his leave, Eduardo could not resist one last barb. "Well," he said, with a mischievous smile, "do not stay away from Florence for too long! We shall miss you, shall we not, Signorina Ashleigh?" He bowed. *"Arrivederci* to you both!" And with a jaunty wave he was gone, striding breezily away along the winding path.

Lucy sat, tense and apprehensive, in the carriage Charles had insisted on hailing for her return to the Castello. Despite his assurances that Count Eduardo's discretion could be relied upon, she was filled with misgiving. If the Contessa were ever to find out about her impropriety, she would be, she knew, in serious trouble. It was highly probable that she would be sent home in disgrace. And the indignity of such an event was as nothing compared to the fact that, if that happened, she would not be able to see Charles Ryman ever again.

Which was why, she had told herself, somewhat menda-

ciously, she had agreed to meet him again the following afternoon.

"I will wait for you here at the same time tomorrow," he
said.

"Very well."

His eyes entreated her. "That is a promise?"

"Yes. A promise."

She had no idea how she would manage another clandestine
meeting, but for the moment, as she drove away, leaving him
standing in the roadside with a hand raised in salute, she did
not care.

Today, she had been shaken to the depths of her being. But
whatever happened, no one, not even the Contessa, would prevent her from seeing Charles again.

Troubled and distracted, she hurried into the Castello through
the side entrance and ran upstairs to her room. She was con-
gratulating herself on having arrived back unseen and had only
just taken off her bonnet and gloves when there was a knock at
her door. She glanced at the mirror at her flushed face and
quickly smoothed her hair. Surely Sofia had not returned home
already.

"Come in!" she called, quickly smoothing her hair.

But it was only Giovanni, wearing an anxious expression.

"La Contessa," he said. "She is waiting to see you in the
salon, *signorina. Molto importante!*"

"I will come at once."

Lucy hurried downstairs, her heart beating fast. There could
only be one reason for this summons. Well, if she had been
found out, she would just have to face up to her great-
grandmother's wrath and tell her the truth.

But when she walked into the salon, she saw at once that the
old lady was merely wearing an expression of kindness and
concern on her lined, aristocratic face.

"Come, my dear, sit down," she said, patting the seat next to
her on the sofa. "I have just received a message with some
news for you from home." She sighed. "I'm afraid you will find
it hard to bear."

Lucy sank down next to her, filled with a new trepidation. "There is something wrong?" The cold hand of fear clutched her heart. "My parents?"

"They are well." The Contessa took her hands in hers. "It is the *bambina*—your little sister. She is sick."

Lucy gave a little gasp. "Antonia? What is it?"

"I am afraid that she has the scarletina. Your parents are very anxious for her."

Lucy, white-faced, stared at the Contessa in horror. Scarletina! She knew what a serious threat this was. Often, the illness was fatal. Only last year there had been an epidemic in Lintern Magna that had resulted in the death of five children. The illness usually began with a sore throat and a high fever with a telltale bright red rash developing within a day or two. Some children were not robust enough to fight the disease and died within days of contracting it.

"How severe is it?" she asked, her voice trembling.

The Contessa sighed. "I will not hide the truth from you, *cara*. The child is very ill. The doctors are doing everything they can. But"—she crossed herself—"she is in God's hands, and we must pray for her."

Lucy had a sudden image of blue-eyed, golden-haired Antonia waving to her and blowing her kisses from her father's arms as she had left for Italy.

Suddenly filled with guilt, she got to her feet with a swift, convulsive movement. While she had been dallying with Charles Ryman in the Rose Garden, her darling little sister had been fighting for her life! It was almost as if this dreadful news was her punishment for behaving in such a reckless and inappropriate manner.

"I must go home," she said. "I had better leave immediately."

"My dear, by the time you arrive, it may already be too late. We must be patient and wait for further news."

"No!" Lucy's eyes filled with tears. "I must go at once. They need me there."

The Contessa put out a restraining hand. "Lucy, please listen to me. It is *impossibile!* We have no way of contacting your friend, Miss Ambrose, and you cannot make the long journey alone. You know that."

"I must!" Lucy turned toward the door. "If Antonia should die, I could never forgive myself for staying here."

Charles Ryman had been pacing in the Giardino delle Rose for almost an hour. The vast array of blooms of every kind and color might have been among the most exquisite in Italy, but Charles, deep in thought, was blind to their beauty.

Several times, his heart lifting, he had looked up expectantly at the sight of some dark-haired young woman—even the appearance of a parasol in the distance—only to have his hopes dashed. But as the minutes passed, he had begun to realize that she had decided not to accept his invitation.

He took out his pocket watch for the third time and sighed. It was probably pointless to wait a moment longer, but he could not bring himself to leave.

He knew that he could not blame her for failing to keep her promise. This was the second time he had asked her to breach the strict code of behavior instilled in her by her refined family. Even if she felt as he did, it was a great deal to expect.

The sleepless night he had spent had left him feeling tense and ill at ease. He had paced the floor until dawn broke upon the dreaming city, telling himself that he was wrong to hope, foolish to imagine that the kind of happiness he had always sought was within his grasp.

Yesterday, when he had kissed her, he had been certain she returned his feelings. And, armed with that knowledge, he had felt that he might put the past behind him. When the time was right, and she knew him better, he would be able to lay down the burden he carried at her feet and beg her to understand and forgive.

Slowly, he continued to pace up and down the path, barely conscious of his surroundings, of the exquisite perfume of the flowers. It was almost five o'clock before he could finally acknowledge the truth. Lucy Ashleigh was not coming to meet him, and there was nothing he could do but accept her decision.

While Charles was waiting for her in the Rose Garden, Lucy was already preparing to make her way home.

The Contessa had insisted that her own personal maid would travel with her, and despite the fact that Maria spoke little English, her kind, stalwart presence would be a great comfort.

Sofia, returning from her visit to Valdarno late that evening, had been in floods of tears when she discovered her cousin preparing to leave.

"The poor little Antonia! I will go with you, *cara!* You must not bear this alone!"

But the Contessa had already arranged for Sofia to go to Genoa later that month to stay with her elder sister, who was expecting her first child. And Sofia had to be content in the knowledge that she would be visiting the Ashleighs the following summer.

"Dearest Lucy! I shall miss you so much!" She had flung her arms around her in her usual extravagant way.

"And I, you." Lucy drew her aside. "There is something I would like you to do for me, Sofia. Something I beg you to keep to yourself. I have written a note, and I wondered whether you could see that this is delivered personally."

She drew the envelope from her journal and handed it to her.

"For Major Ryman!" Sofia's black eyes were now filled with excitement. "Tell me everything!"

"There is very little to tell." Lucy sighed. "I will write to you, Sofia. I promise. But Major Ryman is leaving soon for Rome, and I wanted to explain to him about Antonia. Please see that he gets this today."

"You are in love—I knew it!"

Lucy shook her head and turned away so that her cousin should not see the unshed tears sparkling in her eyes.

Her letter had been brief.

Dear Major Ryman,

I have just heard that my sister is gravely ill, and I must return immediately to England. I am, therefore, unable to keep our rendezvous at the Rose Garden, as we arranged.

I am sorry to have broken a promise, but upon reflection, perhaps it is for the best that we should not meet again. We belong to very different worlds and know so very little about each other.

Forgive me if my behavior yesterday gave rise to any misunderstanding. I can assure you that such conduct is completely out of character for me, and I hope you will not think less of me as a result.

I wish you well in the future.
I remain,

> *Yours most sincerely,*
> *Lucy Ashleigh*

As she took the envelope from her cousin, Sofia, for once, had the sense not to press her for more information.

Lucy was weak with anxiety and dread. The thought of the long and arduous journey by rail, sea, and coach was daunting enough, but to travel knowing that she might be too late to see her beloved little sister was utterly unbearable.

Chapter Six

Lucy never forgot her arrival home from Italy. Horrified by the sight of her parents' weary, despairing faces, she had begged to be allowed to see her little sister, and young Dr. Moorhouse had very reluctantly agreed.

"Any exertion, mental or physical, is dangerous," he said. "The child is in a very precarious state, and she must be kept as quiet as possible."

For several days, Antonia's life had been hanging in the balance, and the doctor held out little hope of a recovery. At first, he had thought that she had contracted the measles, but when her cheeks took on the characteristic flush associated with scarletina, he realized that the illness was even more serious. He had insisted on burning her toys and bed linen for fear of spreading the infection to the other children, and she had been kept in virtual isolation with only her parents and nurses allowed into the sickroom. Her grief-stricken parents had prepared themselves for the worst.

But when Lucy had crept into the room and bent over the little bed, Antonia had looked up. And at the sight of her adored sister bending over her, her eyes had brightened.

"There's my Lucy!" she had whispered, and her little rosebud mouth had curved into a smile.

A few minutes later, she fell into a deep and peaceful sleep. And from then on, her condition had steadily improved. Somehow, the child had fought off the threat of the virulent disease, and the family was convinced that it was the sight of Lucy that had rallied the exhausted little girl.

Her grateful parents were filled with relief and joy, and

when, a month later, the little girl began to trot about the house again, and color started to return to her cheeks, her father decided to remove the family to the coast for a few weeks.

"Some sea air will be good for her and will help the little thing to recuperate," Guy Ashleigh explained to his elder daughter. "The boys can be with us until they return to school at the end of the month, and if the weather is good, we can stay on a little longer. Your stepmother needs the rest, and we are hoping, my love, that you will come with us too."

"Would you mind terribly if I didn't, Papa? I've been away from home for so long that I would like to catch my breath before I go away again. That long journey back . . . I thought it would never end."

"Of course." Her father was disappointed, but he understood. He dropped a kiss onto her head. "We shall miss you, of course. But if you change your mind, you can always join us later."

"My dear, are you sure you really want to stay here by yourself?" her stepmother asked her, slipping her arm through hers as they walked together in the garden later. "Won't you be a little lonely without us?"

Lucy smiled. "No. Grace will be home soon, and I am so looking forward to seeing her. She had missed her best friend, who had been away on a pleasure tour of the Lake District with her husband, Philip Weston, when Lucy had arrived home.

"Of course. Dear Grace! She'll be so pleased to see you." Adeline smiled. "I only asked because I believe that James is at home at the moment, and I wondered whether you would find that a little difficult."

"Not in the least. Being in Italy helped me to put all that behind me. Just as you said it would."

"I'm so glad." Her stepmother glanced at her thoughtfully. Lucy had always been a stoic; she had learned from birth how to accept her lot without complaining, and during her months abroad, she had certainly matured.

But Adeline was surprised by her complete lack of interest in James Wyatt. She had seemed preoccupied lately, as if there was something else on her mind. Even her father had noticed that slight withdrawal, the way she had of appearing to be apart from the family, the slight restraint, even in her laughter. "My love, I don't wish to pry, but I have felt over the past weeks that perhaps there is something worrying you. As if you are still not entirely happy."

For a moment, Lucy hesitated. She wanted very much to confide in her stepmother. The time she had spent with Charles Ryman was now a bittersweet memory, but she could not stop thinking about him, and every day she found herself regretting the note she had sent him. She had written it in a moment of guilt, and she wished with all her heart now that it had not been so formal.

He had never replied to it, although he could easily have obtained her address from Sofia. But she couldn't blame him for that; her tone had been far from encouraging.

Lucy glanced at her stepmother, suddenly longing to unburden herself. But the dark shadows beneath Adeline's eyes were reminders of the ordeal she had so recently been through over little Antonia. The child's illness had taken its toll, and Lucy would not spoil her happiness by burdening her with her own troubles.

Instead, she pressed her arm reassuringly. "I think perhaps I am very tired," she said with perfect truth. And Adeline wisely did not press her to say more.

A few days later, a letter from Sofia arrived. Lucy's heart skipped a beat, and her fingers trembled a little as she opened it. It had been six weeks since she had arrived home from Italy, and the possibility that the contents might contain some passing reference to Charles Ryman brought a sparkle to her eyes.

Sofia had written in English, in purple ink, and her flamboyant handwriting and her quaint, stilted expressions made Lucy smile as she read the contents of the long, rambling account of the latest happenings in Florence.

Sofia's cousin Eduardo had seemed to figure largely in her various exploits, which made Lucy wonder, not for the first time, whether one day the Contessa's hopes might, after all, be fulfilled.

There was no mention of Charles Ryman until the last paragraph.

"So happy to know little Antonia is recovered. Since you have sadly left us, your Major Ryman I have not seen," she wrote. "Eduardo explains that he has left Florence. And soon, he will return to America. Write to me, *cara*, and tell me what is in your heart."

Lucy folded up the sheets of notepaper and felt suddenly desperately lonely. She sat for a long time, alone in her room, deep in thought. She could still conjure up an image of that handsome, patrician face, of those blue eyes, of the bright mane of hair. And it was all too easy to recall the timbre of his voice when he spoke her name, of the strength of his hands holding hers, of the warmth of his lips when he had kissed her in the Rose Garden.

She was deeply in love with him. She had known that then, and she knew it now. The young emotion she had felt for James had been infatuation, hero worship, merely a youthful desire for romance.

If only, she thought, she had been able to see Charles one more time before she left for home. She closed her eyes, shutting out reality, imagining how it might have been. They would be together once more, walking in that beautiful garden. He would tell her again that he loved her, and she would say that, of course, she loved him. And then Charles would return with her to England to meet her family and ask her father's permission to marry her . . .

"Lucy? Are you ready?" Her stepmother's voice, reminding her about their afternoon walk, summoned her back to reality.

"Coming, Mama!" Sadly, she put the letter into her bureau. What use was it to dream? Charles Ryman had gone home to America. The truth was that she could never recapture the happiness of those moments spent with him, and there was no hope of ever seeing him again.

Charles had believed that he had managed to rid himself of the old, recurring nightmare that had troubled his sleep for so many years. But one night soon after he had returned from Rome to Florence, he woke, breathing hard, his forehead wet with perspiration, and realized that the dream had returned to haunt him with renewed power. The same white, ghastly face, the same dark eyes staring sightlessly into his, the feel of cold, smooth metal in his hand, the limp body, twisted in death, lying on the floor.

Heavy-eyed in the dawn, he left his bed and walked across the room to the window. At five o'clock on a fine autumnal morning, with a chill in the air, there was a fine mist rising from the Arno. Charles shivered. Weeks had passed since he had received the curt note from Lucy Ashleigh. Weeks of soul-searching. Of remembering that one perfect moment in the Rose Garden and wondering whether he had been completely mistaken about her feelings for him.

He had been told by Eduardo of Lucy's safe arrival home and had been gladdened by the news of her sister's recovery. But he had lost count of the letters he had written her, letters he had never been able to finish. Again and again, he had reminded himself that she had made her feelings perfectly clear in the brief, cold little note Sofia di Lorenzo had given him. There was no point in pursuing the matter any further.

He should go home, he told himself. Home to the safe anonymity of New York. The dream he'd had of taking Lucy with him as his bride was utterly absurd. Why had he ever dared to imagine that she would want to turn her back on England and all that she loved to go with him? And how could he expect the father who had lost the first ten years of her life to let her go ever again? And to America! With a stranger whose background he would undoubtedly deplore when he knew the truth about him.

It was time that he stopped this foolishness. His business in

Italy was complete, and he had no reason to stay any longer. He needed to visit his London office to tie up a few loose ends, and then he would book a ticket on a passenger ship bound for New York. It would be good to steam down the Hudson River toward the great city he knew and loved and to set foot once again on American soil. He had been in Europe for the best part of a year.

"I have been away too long," he said to Eduardo when he called on him to give him the news of his imminent departure. "But I shall miss Florence and the friends I have made here."

Eduardo regarded him quizzically over the rim of his glass. "And one in particular, perhaps?"

Charles colored slightly. "And who would that be?"

"Oh, come, Charles! Do not treat me like a fool. That afternoon when I saw you in the Rose Garden with Miss Ashleigh—that told me everything."

"Then you were mistaken," Charles said coldly. "Miss Ashleigh and I will not be meeting again. "

"But you are going to England, are you not?"

"Yes, to London for a week or so. For business reasons only."

"And you will not be seeing her?"

"I assure you, my friend, that is not a possibility."

"*E vero.*" Eduardo regarded his friend gravely. "So your feelings are not as deep as I imagined them to be."

"My feelings are my own concern," Charles said brusquely.

"Of course. But permit me to say one more word upon the subject. It is this. If you are saying that you intend to let Lucy Ashleigh go so easily, you must either be a liar . . . or a fool. And I do not believe that you are either."

Chapter Seven

But, Lucy, you promised to come!" Grace Weston stared at her best friend in dismay. "I've been so looking forward to the Hunt Ball. You know how much we always enjoy it. It won't be the same without you!"

"I know, but the thought of it this year fills me with dread. James will be there, and everyone will be watching every move I make and wondering if my broken heart is mended."

"And is it?"

"Yes. Completely."

"Well, then! Why care what anyone else thinks?"

It was an unseasonably warm and sunny autumn afternoon, and the two had walked into Lintern Magna village as they often did when the weather was fine. Although Lucy was six years younger, Grace was her closest friend, and Lucy had been chief bridesmaid at her wedding to Philip Weston two years ago.

They had been very glad to be reunited when Grace returned home from her tour of the Lake Country and had just spent a happy morning together, browsing the latest wares on offer in the village shops. Grace had decided to buy herself a pair of white silk gloves for evening wear at Miss March's Drapery and Dressmaking Emporium, and it was then that the subject of the ball had been aired.

Despite Lucy's reluctance, Grace was determined to persuade her friend to attend.

"I know you might feel awkward at first. But you will be with Philip and me, so you won't have to face all the gossips alone. Besides, you simply can't go on avoiding social occasions forever."

Lucy sighed. Her parents were not due to return until the end of the month, and if they had been with her, she would not have thought twice about attending what was one of the most popular social events of the year. But without their reassuring presence, she felt exposed and vulnerable. *She* might have put her broken romance with James Wyatt behind her, but the rest of Lintern Magna had not. She was quite sure of that. It was some months since she had last accepted an evening invitation or attended a function in England, and although she had returned from Italy she had visited only the few friends she knew she could trust.

"It's too difficult," she said, taking her friend's arm as they walked across the village green, skirting the duck pond and the cricket pitch, which had been carefully fenced off at the end of the season. "I hate the thought of coming face-to-face with James and his parents. Perhaps it's cowardly of me, but I'm afraid it's the truth."

"It's not cowardly at all. I don't blame you in the least." Grace was so agitated that she almost dropped her chenille-fringed parasol. "But it's not you who should feel bad about what happened. I think the Wyatts behaved despicably, and I know that my brother George thinks exactly the same. Everyone knows what snobs they are, and Isabel is the worst of them all—even if she is George's wife!"

Lucy nodded. James' older married sister, Isabel, was a force to be reckoned with. She had made no secret of her disapproval of the prospect of his marriage to Lucy.

"And as for James . . ." Grace began.

"No." Lucy frowned. "I bear James no ill will, and I shall always be fond of him. Yes, truly. You see, I know now that what we felt for each other was little more than affection between two longtime friends. If we had really loved each other, nothing could have stood in our way."

"Really?"

"Yes, really." Lucy, suddenly realizing that what she had said might equally apply to Charles Ryman and herself, smiled rather ruefully. "I promise you, I no longer hanker after him. Italy cured me of that."

Grace gave her friend a shrewd glance. "Italy? Or something else?"

Lucy colored faintly, and she kept her glance firmly ahead. "I wish you could have been there with me, Grace. Florence is so beautiful."

"And, I've heard, extremely romantic." Grace stopped walking, forcing her friend to turn and face her. "I think something happened there. Something you haven't mentioned. Lucy, did you meet some handsome young Italian nobleman? Tell me at once!"

Lucy smiled. "I met several handsome young Italian noblemen."

"And there was one in particular, wasn't there?" Grace examined her friend's face and gave a sigh. "I knew it!"

Lucy hesitated. She had been longing to confide in someone ever since she had arrived home, and more than once she had been on the brink of telling Grace about Charles. "I did meet someone," she said at last, casting caution to the winds. "But he wasn't Italian. He was from New York."

"Really? An American! How interesting!"

"I met him through Sofia at a soiree at the Castello. He was a friend of her cousin Eduardo."

Grace nodded, her eyes intent on her friend's face. "Go on!"

"There is really very little to tell." Grace was her dearest friend, but she was now a staid married woman and inclined to be prim. Unlike Sofia, who had encouraged her cousin to flirt, she would have been horrified if she knew that Lucy had actually allowed herself to be kissed.

But something in Lucy's manner had obviously aroused her curiosity. "His name?"

"Ryman. Major Charles Ryman. He was . . . is charming."

"And handsome, no doubt."

"Very." Lucy could not quite look her friend in the eye. "We only met a few times, but we . . . I liked him very much."

"Really?" Grace was fascinated.

"Yes, but it is foolish of me to go on thinking about him, because I am not likely to see him ever again. You see, when

I heard that Antonia was sick, I had to leave Florence without saying good-bye. And by now, he will probably have returned to America."

"I do not mean to sound unkind, Lucy," Grace said after a pause, "but perhaps it is for the best. It might be a little hasty to become involved with someone you know so little about. And he is, after all, a foreigner."

But Lucy wasn't listening. She sighed. "I was sure he liked me. But I must have been wrong."

"Really?" Grace looked faintly relieved.

"Yes. I wrote to him before I left Florence to tell him about Antonia. I'm sure that if he wished to communicate with me, he would have done so by now."

Struck by the woebegone expression on Lucy's face, Grace took her hand.

"Lucy, dear, are you sure that what you felt for this man was not infatuation? Is there really no hope that you and James might somehow find a way to overcome your difficulties?"

"None whatsoever." The look in Lucy's eyes was uncompromising. "Even if it was possible, I would never marry him. His parents were right to have prevented the match. Perhaps they did so for the wrong reasons, but I realize now that I have cause to be grateful to them."

Grace looked bewildered. "How can that be?"

"Because you see," Lucy said, suddenly overcome with emotion, "when I met Charles Ryman, I understood for the first time what is was to feel . . . well . . . passion."

Grace, shocked by such an admission, averted her eyes. It was absolutely not appropriate to discuss such indelicate matters, even among close friends.

"Lucy dear," she said gently, "I think perhaps the atmosphere in Florence might have gone to your head a little. I'm certain this Major Ryman is all that you say he is, but in time you will realize that it was merely a brief infatuation."

Lucy shook her head. "I shall never forget our time together," she said. "But I know that I cannot go on thinking about him. I won't let myself be miserable a second time. I must try to be grateful for my wonderful family and friends and enjoy life as much as possible."

If Grace was unconvinced by the resolute expression on her friend's face, she did not show it.

"In that case," she said cheerfully, "you really must come to the ball. If you do not, you will be sorely missed. In fact, if you refuse, I shall tell Philip that I shan't attend either."

Lucy laughed. "That would be foolish, and you know it!"

Grace was utterly devoted to her dashing young husband, who was a prominent member of the hunting set. She found it difficult to deny him anything, let alone deprive him of the pleasure of her company at the ball.

"Then change your mind and come!" Grace said. "It is time you stopped hiding, Lucy. Because you have nothing at all to be ashamed of."

Lucy was silent for a moment. Then she sighed. "Well, I can never again feel at ease in the company of the Wyatts. But you are right, it would be foolish to keep on hiding away. After all, I am not the first girl to be cast aside. Most people know my history and think no worse of me, and I am not ashamed of my mother's humble origins. It is not a crime to be poor."

Grace pressed her friend's arm, beaming with pleasure. "I knew you would be sensible. And now we can make plans and discuss what we shall wear." She sighed. "Dear Lucy, it is so lovely to have my best friend back! I was beginning to think she had gone forever."

The Hunt Ball was one of the most important events in the village's social calendar. This year, it was to take place at the Assembly Rooms at Lintern Magna, and as it was Lucy's first public engagement for almost a year, she was determined to look her best. Before Grace had married, she and Lucy would often choose ball dresses in matching styles and colors, but the latest fashion dictated that, this year, young, unmarried ladies should wear dresses made of light materials, worn over silk slips.

Grace would wear white satin, as befitted her married status, and Lucy, having thought long and hard about her own attire, had chosen one of the gowns she'd had made for her by the Contessa's couturier in Italy.

Simple and elegant, it was made of Ottoman satin trimmed with tulle, and the deep shade of turquoise blue had been much admired in Florence. She had needed new accessories for the evening, of course, and Grace had advised her to wear the delicate ankle boots designed for her by a Florentine shoemaker. They were made of satin in a color two or three shades paler than her gown and were at present considered to be the very height of European fashion.

She wore white flowers in her hair and a silver locket that had belonged to her grandmother on a fine chain around her neck. Her arrival turned heads. Even more fascinating than the fact that she was there was the elegance of her appearance. When she had left for Italy, she had been known to be a sweet, shy, rather diffident girl. She had returned, a few months later, a poised young woman.

No one, not even Grace, could have guessed at her inner turmoil, at her longing to turn around and escape when she emerged from the ladies' dressing room into a scene vibrant with music and laughter.

She looked around the room with its ornate domed ceiling and highly polished oak floor. The brilliant scene—the ladies fluttering like a swarm of brightly colored butterflies across the dance floor, the men in tails and white ties, interspersed with the scarlet coats of senior members of the Hunt—was lit by a magnificent chandelier consisting of thousands of pieces of hand-cut crystal. There was certainly no hiding place here!

Smiling as she acknowledged the greetings of friends and neighbors, and acutely aware of the mixture of pity and sympathy in many of the looks bestowed upon her, she moved gracefully across the room with Philip and Grace at her side.

There were some, she knew, who reveled in the faintest aura of gossip circulating in the village. But there were also those, like Grace's parents, Lord and Lady Hardwicke, who welcomed her back and treated her with the same warmth and friendliness as ever. And Lucy was determined to ignore the few who thoroughly enjoyed the misfortunes of others and made no secret of it.

"How positively brave of you, dear, to come tonight!" whispered Mrs Oliver-Pritchard, one of the more poisonous of the village busybodies.

"Plenty more fish in the sea, what?" thundered her large, well-meaning, red-faced husband. "Good-looking young girl like you . . ." And then he stopped, suddenly aware of his wife's repressive look.

Having thankfully escaped their clutches, Lucy turned to find herself face-to-face with the Wyatt party. It was a large group that included several guests, among them a sulky, auburn-haired young woman who seemed to be regarding her with considerable interest.

Acutely aware of the look of agony on James' face as his dark eyes met hers, she stopped to acknowledge their perfunctory greetings, her expression impassive. His parents moved on quickly without introducing their friends, but his sister, Isabel Hardwicke, nodded coldly.

"So you have finally returned from Europe," she said, her green eyes hostile. "We did not expect to see you, of all people, here tonight."

"Really?" Lucy stood her ground. "Why not?"

"Why not, indeed!" George Hardwicke shot his wife a warning look. "It's delightful to see you, Lucy. Your father tells me you enjoyed your visit to Florence."

"Very much!"

Isabel stared at her. "Where *is* Guy?" she demanded. "It's not like him to miss a Hunt Ball."

Lucy returned her icy glance with disdain. "My parents are away. They have taken the children to Weymouth for the sea air."

Isabel made a face. "Really? Poor Guy. I had no idea he took his domestic duties so seriously."

"Lucy, may I introduce my friend Mr. Fielding?" Philip, his kind brown eyes noting the flush of anger rising in Lucy's face, stepped quickly into the breach to prevent a further exchange. "I'm afraid he simply refuses to leave me in peace until he has made your acquaintance."

The next moment she was in the arms of an eager young man with bright red hair, who broke all the rules by flirting with her outrageously. And her attention was claimed in quick succession by several other admirers eager to place their names on her card. George Hardwicke made a point of asking her to dance the polka and whirled her cheerfully around the dance floor, blithely ignoring the outraged expressions of his wife and mother-in-law. He was a close friend of her father's and had watched Lucy grow from a little lost child into the poised young woman she now was.

"I am happy to see you return safe and well," he said, as he escorted her back to her seat. "You have been sorely missed, as I'm certain my little sister has already told you."

And soon, swept along by the music and convivial atmosphere, Lucy began to forget her earlier anxieties, and she was glad that she had made the effort to be present.

It was early evening and bitterly cold as the carriage set down the solitary passenger at The Golden Lion Inn at Lintern Magna.

"Thank you kindly, sir." The coachman set down his valises and caught the coin that was tossed him. "They'll make you comfortable here, I promise you."

"Good. Thanks for your help." The tall figure turned to look up at the half-timbered building with the brightly painted sign depicting a lion rampant hanging over the broad oak door.

As the carriage drove away, he stepped inside. There was a sudden silence as he walked into the cozy taproom where a few of the locals were sitting near the open fire with their pewter tankards of ale before them on the scarred wooden tables.

Several pairs of eyes examined the newcomer with a curiosity tinged with hostility. They noted the cut and cloth of his dark blue frock coat and narrow black trousers, the silk cravat with its heavy gold pin, and the fine leather of his boots. But if the stranger was aware of their animosity, he gave no sign of it. Tall, broad-shouldered, with the look about him of a man who would not walk away from a fight, he returned their stares coolly and then turned to the landlord's apple-cheeked wife behind the polished oak bar.

"I'd like to take a room, please," Charles Ryman said.

"Certainly, sir," she said, dimpling at him. "For just the one night?"

"I'm not quite sure."

"That's all right, sir," She reached for a key from the set on the wall behind her. "If you'd like to come this way . . ."

As he followed her up the narrow, twisting staircase, conversation resumed in the bar, and he distinctly heard the word "foreigner." No doubt, he thought, wryly, that term would apply to anyone who had not been born and bred in the neighborhood.

The room he was shown to was small but spotlessly clean, and most of the space was taken up by a vast bed piled high with bolster and pillows and covered with a patchwork quilt.

He had been forced to bend his knees to get through the door, and the low-beamed ceiling was equally challenging.

"Can I get you some supper, sir? There's a nice piece of beefsteak and kidney pie. Or perhaps you'd prefer the mutton hot pot?"

He shook his head. "Thank you, but I've already dined," he said. "Maybe later, I will have some bread and cheese with a glass of your best ale."

Then, as she turned to go, he said, "Tell me, would you know of a gentleman called Ashleigh? I believe he lives in the neighborhood."

The landlady laughed. "Know him, sir? Why, he's our Squire! When old Sir Roderick, his uncle, was alive, I was in service at the Manor."

"Would you be kind enough to direct me there in the morning?"

"Gladly, sir. But you won't find Sir Guy or Lady Ashleigh in residence. They have gone to the seaside with their little ones.

Miss Lucy, now—that's their eldest—she's at home. She'll be at the Hunt Ball tonight."

"I see."

"Such a big occasion it is, sir. This year, they've held it in the Assembly Rooms in the village. All the gentry will be there, the ladies in their beautiful gowns and the gentlemen in their hunting scarlet."

He nodded. "Thank you for the information. By the way," he added as he followed her downstairs, "in the morning, I will need a horse. Perhaps you could tell me where I can find the nearest livery stable."

"You see? I was right!" Grace said as, flushed from their exertions on the dance floor, she and Lucy went to the refreshment room for ices. "I knew you would enjoy yourself! I'm so glad you came! Everyone is so delighted to see you."

"Apart from the Wyatts, of course."

"Fiddlesticks! Who cares what they think?"

"True. It was kind of your brother to ask me to dance."

"George," Grace said, "is a dear. I have three brothers, and I love them all. But he is my favorite. But as for his wife . . ." She left the sentence unfinished.

Lucy frowned. "I hate the proprietary way in which Isabel always refers to my father and never mentions my stepmother."

"You must pay no attention to her. I certainly don't!" She turned from the mirror and smiled at Lucy. "Shall we return to the fray? I see that you still have several names on your card, and you mustn't disappoint any of them!"

The worst was over, Lucy thought, as they made their way back to the ballroom. It was highly unlikely that she would encounter the Wyatts face-to-face again. And then, at that precise moment, she looked up to find James approaching her.

His handsome, high-colored face wore an expression of extreme embarrassment, and he was not quite able to look her in the eye.

She colored slightly but stood her ground as he made her a bow.

"Will you honor me with the next dance, Miss Ashleigh?" he asked formally.

Lucy, disguising her amazement, looked up at him calmly. "Thank you, but I am already engaged."

"Then may I place my name on your card?"

"Of course." Lucy knew that it was not proper for a lady to refuse if she was approached in the correct manner. Besides, embarrassed as she was, she bore James no ill will, and she could see how much it had cost him to approach her, with his disapproving family looking on.

He signed her card with a slightly unsteady hand. "Thank you," he said, and he stepped away as she was whisked off into a quadrille.

Lucy told herself later that she had merely imagined that there was a short but significant cessation of talk and laughter in the room when James appeared at her side to claim her. As he led her into the slow waltz, however, it was not mere fancy but fact that their appearance together engaged the attention of almost everyone in the room.

Lucy forced herself to smile when he put his arm around her waist and took her right hand. Her whole body was rigid with self-consciousness. Once—and now it seemed such a very long time ago—she had been proud and happy to dance with James. But now, every second was pure torture.

When he bent his head to speak to her, she kept her face averted.

"Lucy"—his voice was almost a whisper—"I know you must hate the sight of me, and I don't in the least blame you, but . . ."

"I don't hate you, James. I promise you. What happened is in the past."

He sighed. "I asked you to dance because I could think of no other way to speak to you privately."

Lucy shook her head. "I'd rather you didn't, James. There is really nothing to say."

He pressed her hand, forcing her to look up at him.

"But there is. I have something important to tell you. Just hear me out." His voice was growing louder, more urgent, and he was clutching her hand much too tightly. "I had no idea that you would be here tonight, and I really need to explain . . ."

"Please, don't!"

Desperate to get her attention and seemingly oblivious to those close to them on the crowded floor, James, steering her into a turn, suddenly lost his concentration.

The next moment, they had collided painfully with another couple, and as they staggered to keep their balance, a large foot stepped backward on the hem of Lucy's gown.

The culprit, a red-faced young man, looked around at her, horrified. "I do beg your pardon, madam," he said. "Are you hurt?"

Then, when she shook her head and forced a smile, he turned upon James. "Good Lord, man! Can't you look where you are going?" And with a scowl, he swept his partner back into the dance.

"I'm sorry. That was so clumsy of me." James stared down at her in dismay. "Are you sure you're not hurt?"

"Quite sure. But we had better leave the floor." Lucy had heard an ominous tearing noise after they had collided. "I'm afraid my gown has been torn."

"But I need to talk to you . . ."

"I'm sorry. I must go and have it attended to."

And James, his face suffused with misery, was forced to escort Lucy across the room and watch helplessly while Grace accompanied her to the ladies' dressing room.

"You poor thing!" Grace said, as one of the maids in the dressing room examined the hem of Lucy's gown. "What was James thinking? He should have been protecting you from a collision!"

"It might have been worse." The damage to the hem was not extensive, and the temporary repair took only a few minutes.

"At least," Lucy said, "it meant that I could escape from James."

"Really?" Grace sighed. "I was so hoping that you and James might somehow have found a way to overcome your difficulties. It would have been lovely to be related to you, if only by marriage."

Lucy smiled. "You know very well that's no longer possible."

As they made their way back to their table, they suddenly realized that the band had stopped playing. People were standing around the edges of the dance floor, and there seemed to be a general air of expectancy.

"What is happening? Why has everything stopped?" Grace asked her husband as they joined him.

"Apparently, there is about to be some kind of announcement," Philip said. "The Master of Ceremonies has called for silence."

As he finished speaking, Lord Wyatt got to his feet and came forward. A striking-looking man with silver gray hair and a proud, aristocratic face, he stood, resplendent in his scarlet tailcoat, looking around him until there was complete silence.

"My lords, ladies, and gentlemen," he began. "Let me begin by saying how delightful it is to see so many of our hunting fraternity and their guests here tonight. I'm sure we are all delighted by the continuing success of this occasion. Tonight, I have an important announcement to make that gives me— and my family—a particular reason for celebration. As many of you who attended the occasion will remember, in December of last year, on the twentieth of the month, to be exact, my eldest son, James, attained his majority. As my heir, he assumed responsibility for the running of the Wyatt estates."

During the polite applause that broke out at this juncture, Lucy found herself glancing at James, who was standing just behind his father, next to the young woman Lucy had noticed earlier. He was staring straight ahead, his face set and expressionless, and suddenly Lucy began to feel distinctly uneasy as the possibilities of what might happen next began to occur to her.

"As you will all agree," Lord Wyatt went on, "every young man about to make his way in life may carry out his duties much more effectively if he has at his side the support and comfort of a loyal and devoted wife."

Amid the murmurs of assent and cheers, Lucy willed herself to look calm, praying that she would not betray for a single second her discomfort. She knew now what James had meant to tell her. She must have been the last person that he had expected to see there tonight and had been horrified when he saw her arrive. He had tried his best to save her feelings, and it was too late now to wish she had allowed him to speak. It had been sheer vanity that had made her to think he was trying to explain that he was still in love with her! She was grateful to feel Grace's hand gripping hers as she struggled to look calm and unconcerned.

"It therefore gives me great pleasure to announce the engagement of our eldest son to Lady Dorothea, the only daughter of Lord Fitzallan of Bridgenorth, who has kindly given his permission for the match. He is at present abroad but will be joining us to celebrate Christmas."

He waited for the polite applause to die down before continuing. "The marriage will take place in London, on the fifteenth of April, at St. Paul's Cathedral." Turning to smile at the young couple, he raised his glass.

"James and Dorothea! Health and happiness to you both!"

As the toast was echoed around the room, Lucy remained very still, gazing ahead, seemingly oblivious to the whispers and glances of those around her. But she missed nothing, particularly the look of amused contempt bestowed upon her by Isabel Hardwicke.

"Come and sit down," Grace murmured, slipping her arm through hers. The band had resumed playing, and couples began to move toward the dance floor. "I'm so sorry, Lucy. I had no idea that this was happening. I should never have persuaded you to come. I cannot understand why George didn't say anything."

"It really doesn't matter. I am happy for James, and that is the truth." The trouble was, apart from Grace, Lucy thought, no one knew that, and so she was forced to endure their pity and, in some cases, their derision.

"Well, I wish them joy," Grace said flatly. "But Lady Dorothea can't hold a candle to you, can she, Philip?"

"Grace, please!" Lucy said, embarrassed.

"As usual," Philip said, "my darling wife is quite right. But people will say that James has done well for himself. His fiancée is the only child of a very wealthy man who owns half of Norfolk."

"Yes," Grace said. "And, knowing the Wyatts, James probably had no choice in the matter." She looked at her friend anxiously. "Would you like us to have the carriage brought 'round? I would be quite happy to go home."

"No, of course not. The music is about to start up again, and it is time you danced with your husband."

Grace smiled. "I think Philip has had his fill of dancing. He'd be quite happy to leave, and so would I."

Lucy, sorely tempted, hesitated. But as she was about to answer, her heart leaped into her throat. There, striding across the room, was a tall man with a mane of bright golden hair. There was a touch of arrogance in his manner, and he had a careless ease of bearing that was clearly natural to him. His blue eyes sparkled as his glance fell upon Lucy, and he came toward her with a smile that lit up his handsome face.

For a moment, Lucy, utterly astonished, thought that what she was seeing was merely an illusion.

But the hand that took hers was warm and solid and reassuring.

Charles Ryman bowed. "May I have the honor of dancing with you, Miss Ashleigh?"

And, without waiting for an answer, he swept her into his arms and into the waltz.

Chapter Eight

There was no doubt about it: Charles Ryman's sudden appearance had caused a minor sensation, and people were craning their necks to get a closer look. To begin with, he was not wearing evening dress—a serious breach of etiquette—but, judging from his ease of bearing, he obviously did not care. Against this formal and correct background, he stood out like some glamorous and exotic character from a storybook.

They were playing Strauss, "The Blue Danube," and Lucy, still trembling from the shock of his sudden appearance, gazed up at him, spellbound. Neither of them spoke a word, but the expression in their eyes as they looked at each other said everything. Her head was thrown back, her lips were parted, her eyes as bright as stars. And she danced with him as if she was in a trance, oblivious to everything, conscious only of the nearness of him, of the texture of the fine broadcloth of his coat beneath her gloved fingers, of the gentle pressure of his hand in the small of her back, of the clean, sharp scent of his cologne. As she surrendered herself to the rhythm of the music, she wished she could have stayed in his arms for the rest of the evening, and perhaps beyond it.

When, finally, the waltz ended, they stood, for a few moments, still entwined, still oblivious to their surroundings.

"I can't believe you are here," she whispered at last. "I thought you had returned to New York."

"I meant to," he said. "But I couldn't leave without saying good-bye."

Suddenly conscious of the fascinated glances of those around them, she freed herself gently and stepped away.

"I never imagined that I would be seeing you again."

"When you didn't come to meet me at the Rose Garden, neither did I."

"But I wrote to you to explain," Lucy said quickly.

"I didn't receive your letter until I returned from Rome some weeks later. I was very glad to hear from Eduardo that your sister had made a full recovery."

"It was such a very great relief. Antonia is the darling of the family. We all adore her."

"If she at all resembles you," he said, "I am not in the least surprised."

She smiled at him tremulously. Suddenly, there was magic in the air. Everything about this man beguiled her—his looks, his voice, his touch. And he had come all this way to see her again!

"How did you know where to find me?" she asked. His presence still seemed utterly unreal.

"It wasn't difficult. When I arrived, I put up at The Golden Lion." He smiled. "I merely asked for directions to Lintern Manor and was not only told that the Squire was away from home but that his elder daughter could be found here at the Hunt Ball."

"I'm afraid there is very little privacy in an English village," she said. And then her smile froze as, out of the corner of her eye, she caught sight of Isabel Hardwicke drifting past them with George, her slanting green eyes glittering with speculation.

"Shall we sit down?" Charles asked, and he offered her his arm.

Halfway across the room, they came face-to-face with the very couple Lucy would have wished to avoid. James Wyatt must have felt equally averse to the confrontation and turned his head away, pretending he hadn't noticed them. But his fiancée half stopped, her eyes widening with the shock of recognition, and Charles bowed.

"Lady Dorothea."

But even as his lips formed the name, James swept her past, and they disappeared through the throng.

Lucy, startled by the brief exchange, looked at Charles, who was still gazing after them. "How amazing that you should meet someone you know," she said, as they walked on. "Here! Of all places!"

"Yes." He frowned. The encounter seemed to have ruffled him. "We met last summer. I was invited to shoot on her father's estate in Norfolk. A strange coincidence!"

"She has just become engaged."

"Really? Was that her fiancé with her?"

"Yes. James. James Wyatt."

Lucy turned away, hoping he wouldn't notice the sudden color in her cheeks. It had been an awkward moment, and this was not the time or the place to explain.

Grace watched, fascinated, as her friend was escorted from the dance floor by the handsome stranger.

She was not the only person in the room to have been struck by his sudden arrival, but, unlike everyone else, she had no shadow of a doubt as to his identity. This man could not possibly be anyone but the American Lucy had met in Florence, Major Charles Ryman. And if his arrival had caused a stir, their appearance together on the dance floor had been even more riveting. The careful formality of their execution of the slow waltz had been impeccable. But the fact that they were deeply attracted to each other had been obvious to Grace and probably to everyone else in the room.

Small wonder, Grace thought, as she and Philip exchanged significant glances, that Lucy's affair with James Wyatt had become a thing of the past. Major Ryman would set any woman's heart aflutter!

"What brings you to this part of the world, Major?" Philip asked, after the introductions were made.

Charles smiled. "I had some unfinished business to attend to," he said, and Grace did not miss the quick glance he exchanged with Lucy. "And Miss Ashleigh has spoken so warmly about the delights of Devonshire that I thought it was time I saw it for myself."

"I hope you are not disappointed," Grace said.

"No, indeed. Quite the contrary. I left London early this morning by train, and the journey gave me the chance to enjoy your beautiful countryside."

"But surely Devonshire can't compare with Italy!"

"I disagree. Italy has its charms, but at the moment"—he did not look at Lucy, but the inference was perfectly clear—"I would rather be here than anywhere else in the world."

A wave of color flooded her cheeks at his words, and Grace came quickly to the rescue.

"You are staying in the neighborhood, Major Ryman?" she asked.

"I have taken temporary lodgings at The Golden Lion, which is where I was given directions to find Miss Ashleigh."

"This is one of our most popular annual events," Philip explained. "Do you hunt, Major Ryman?"

He nodded. "I used to ride out regularly with the Belvedere in New York. But these days I am traveling far too much to be able to hunt as often as I'd like."

"Then I hope you are staying long enough to ride with the Lintern," Philip said. "I can accommodate you at my stables and find you a decent mount if you like."

"That is most civil of you, sir. I'd very much enjoy that."

"And, of course, you must come and dine with us very soon!" Grace said, with a glance at Lucy.

"I shall look forward to it."

"Excellent! The next meet is Tuesday week, I believe," Philip said. "So we must hope to see you before then." He turned to his wife. "And now, my love, if you do not object, I must confess to have had enough dancing for one evening. Are you two ladies ready to leave?"

Grace glanced at Lucy and saw the unspoken appeal in her eyes. "Not quite. Just one more waltz, please, Philip. And then, if Lucy agrees, we shall set off for home."

"Your friends seem very pleasant," Charles said, as Philip led his wife into the dance.

Lucy smiled. "I am very fond of them both. Grace and I are almost like sisters. I missed her very much when I went to Italy."

"Although you had your cousin, Signorina Sofia, for company."

"Yes, and she is a dear. But they are quite different. Grace is very sensible, and Sofia tends to be more . . . impulsive."

She looked up quickly as James and his fiancée waltzed past. Surely she was not imagining the hostile glance Lady Dorothea gave them.

"Do you know Dorothea Fitzallan well?" Charles asked, as if he, too, had noticed it.

"Not at all. I saw her for the first time tonight."

Her voice faltered, and Charles glanced at her quickly. "Could her fiancé be the man you mentioned to me in Florence?"

Lucy drew in her breath sharply. She had forgotten how direct and outspoken Charles was. "Yes. Their engagement was announced tonight."

He gave her a solicitous glance. "A difficult moment?"

"Only rather a surprise. I hope they will be very happy."

"And so now," he said, "you can put the past behind you and begin again."

She smiled. "Yes, to a certain extent. You see, James and I belong to the same set. James' eldest sister, Isabel, is married to Grace's brother George. And George is my father's oldest friend." She gave a breathless little laugh at the expression of bewilderment on Charles' face. "I'm afraid it is all rather complicated."

He laughed. "No doubt, if I stay here long enough, I might begin to grasp it."

She glanced at him quickly. "And how long do you intend to stay?"

"That rather depends upon you." He held her startled glance. "I was hoping to call on you tomorrow."

Lucy hesitated. With her parents still at Weymouth, it would not be correct for her to receive a male guest alone in their absence.

"In England, it's not really considered proper to call without first leaving a card," she began. "And my parents are away." But out of the corner of her eye she saw Grace and Philip approaching and decided to cast caution to the winds. "But, since we are already acquainted . . ."

"Then I look forward to it." He got to his feet with a smile as Grace appeared at his elbow.

"We have come to collect Miss Ashleigh," she said, "and to bid you good night, Major Ryman."

"Unless, Major, you are also ready to leave," Philip said. "In which case, we can offer you a seat in our carriage. We pass The Golden Lion on our way home."

Sitting next to Charles Ryman in the carriage seemed to Lucy like some strange but wonderful dream. The Westons were clearly fascinated as they made polite inquiries about Charles' business interests, his home in New York, and his travel in Europe. On his part, he showed considerable interest in the local area and seemed interested in the price of land and property in and around Lintern Magna.

Lucy was receiving silent messages from Grace, who was sitting opposite and communicating with her eyes. They often did this when they were in company and wished to share some private jest. But now her expression was serious rather than mischievous, and Lucy knew that later she would want answers to her unspoken questions.

For her part, Lucy was too overwrought and emotional to play the game. Obliged to cling to the edge of her seat as the carriage swayed and jolted over a muddy pothole in the road, she had suddenly felt the tips of Charles' fingers against the inside of her wrist. And although the coach had righted itself, neither of them chose to break the delicate contact. His touch had rendered her blind and deaf to everything else, and she both longed for and dreaded the moment when the short journey would come an end.

When, at The Golden Lion, the step was let down and Charles bid them good night, with promises to call upon them very soon, his smile was for Lucy and her alone. And her skin went on tingling from his touch as they set off again toward Ashleigh Manor.

"So that," Grace said, after the briefest of pauses, "is your Major Ryman!"

Lucy cast an embarrassed glance at Philip. "Excuse me," she said hastily, "he is not 'my' anything!"

"Perhaps not," Grace said, "but I can quite understand why you found your stay in Italy so pleasant. He is handsome and charming, and his accent is delightful! Don't you agree, Philip?"

But her husband was not in the least interested in the Major's personal attributes. He shrugged. "I'll wager he has a good seat on a horse," he said. "These cavalrymen ride as if they were born in the saddle. I think Caesar would be the right mount for him. He takes some handling, but I have the feeling the Major will be more than a match for the young devil."

"Oh, Philip, really!" Grace shook her head. "As if Lucy cares about that!" She turned back to her friend. "It must have been such a shock for you when he suddenly walked in!"

"I could hardly believe my eyes. I never imagined I would see him again. And certainly not here, at home!"

Grace gave her a faintly anxious look. "I hope you don't mind my saying this, Lucy dear, but he is a little . . . unconventional, don't you think?"

Lucy laughed. "Perhaps that is why I like him so much."

"But to march into the Assembly Rooms quite unannounced! And not even in evening dress! Why, it's unheard of!"

"I suppose so." Lucy's smile was a little forced as she caught the note of criticism in Grace's voice. What did it matter what Charles had been wearing? He had still been far and away the most handsome man in the room, and he had come to find her, not to attend the ball. It had been the most extraordinary evening—so utterly unexpected from beginning to end. The announcement of James' engagement had been startling enough, but it had faded into insignificance upon the arrival of Charles Ryman.

Lucy would never forget the shock and delight she had felt

at the sight of him walking toward her across the ballroom. The utter bliss of dancing in the circle of his arms had blocked, temporarily, her awareness of the presence of everyone else in the room. Until, that is, the moment when she had come face-to-face with James and his fiancée and had noticed the effect of the brief exchange between Charles and Lady Dorothea Fitzallan.

Something told her that there was meaning in the look that had passed between them. And although she tried to dismiss it, a faint feeling of disquiet lingered in the back of Lucy's mind. There were a thousand questions she longed to discuss with Grace, but the presence of Philip made any intimate conversation impossible.

It was much later, when her maid had left her and Lucy was ready for bed, that she allowed herself to reflect upon the exact reasons for Charles' presence. Surely he had not come all this way merely to say good-bye!

The early-morning mist was beginning to dissipate as Charles Ryman cantered down the dusty white road that skirted the village. The stableman at the livery watched his retreating figure with some admiration. This man knew how to handle a horse. His muscular body moved in such perfect harmony with his mount that they looked as if they were part of the same magnificent machine.

When he reached the track leading up over the moor, Charles let the mare have her head, and with the tail and mane streaming out behind, they flew like an arrow across the springy turf.

He felt his inner tension drain from him at the powerful rhythm of the hooves thundering beneath him, and he did not draw rein until they reached a high vantage point protected by an outcropping of gray rocks.

There beneath him, in the green valley below, was the castellated manor house that was the home of Lucy Ashleigh. The ancient building was larger and even more impressive than he had expected.

Built of silver-gray limestone, its heavily mullioned windows peered out from ivy-clad walls across a garden planted with azaleas and hydrangeas, white and gold and blue. And in the center of the manicured lawn stood a huge and ancient mulberry tree.

So this, then, Charles thought, was the cherished home Lucy had so lovingly described for him on that first day. A family home, despite its overwhelming sense of centuries of tradition and history. And as his eyes took in its beauty, he felt his heart sink. He had come to England filled with hope and determination to ask Lucy to be his wife. He had told himself that he could offer her a great deal—wealth, luxury, travel—everything her heart could desire. But how could he match this? How could he ask her to give up her birthright? To give up everything she had known and loved for a home in a foreign country among strangers?

But still, something in her eyes as she had looked at him last night gave him hope. And as he turned to ride back to the inn, he knew that he would not leave England without asking her to go with him.

With the limits of calling hours formally fixed between three o'clock and six, Lucy was shocked at eleven that morning when the butler announced the arrival of a gentleman caller.

"A Major Ryman to see you, Miss Lucy. Shall I say that you are unable to receive visitors at this hour?"

Lucy, sitting in the morning room writing a letter to Sofia, jumped to her feet, brushing back her hair, which hung loose about her face. "Yes—I mean . . . no!" She gave a frantic glance at the gilt-framed mirror over the mantelpiece. Callers never came unexpectedly in the morning, and Charles Ryman had caught her completely off guard. She was wearing one of her oldest and shabbiest gowns, and she knew that she was not fit to be seen in polite company. But she could not send him away. "You may send Major Ryman in, thank you, Rawlings," she said, trying to sound calm and dignified.

"Very well, miss." And with an extremely disapproving expression, he ushered Charles Ryman into the room.

"Good morning!" he said. "I hope this is not an inconvenient time."

"No, not all." She looked defiantly at the manservant, who was hovering. "Thank you, Rawlings. Would you please bring us some tea?"

"Very good, Miss Lucy."

And when, with a reproachful glance, he had closed the door behind him, she turned to her guest. "I'm afraid I wasn't expecting you so early."

"Yet another breach of etiquette!" Charles said with a rueful smile. "Forgive me. I shall try to do better."

She blushed. "It's just that I'm not dressed to receive visitors."

"You look charming." His eyes were eloquent. "You always look charming, which is only one of the reasons I cannot stop thinking about you."

Lucy turned away, flustered. "Please," she said, "won't you sit down? The tea will be here soon. But perhaps I should have asked Rawlings to bring coffee. We don't drink coffee until after dinner, but I've heard that Americans prefer it." She knew she sounded incoherent, but it was impossible to stop. "I can ask Rawlings to bring you coffee if you wish. Or perhaps you'd prefer wine. Do you care for Madeira? My father sometimes takes a glass—he says it's good for him, and I'm sure he's right, so if—"

"No," he interrupted gently, smiling at her. "Thank you, just some tea." He glanced around him appreciatively at the oak-paneled walls and elegant furnishings. "You have a very beautiful home."

"We think so."

He stood with his hands behind his back and leaned forward to look carefully at the portrait of a beautiful, dark-haired, dark-eyed woman that hung over the mantel. "Surely that is a Bellini?"

"Yes. It is called *A Florentine Lady*."

"It's very fine."

"It has been in the family for almost two hundred years. She is believed to be a di Lorenzo."

He nodded. "There is certainly a family resemblance. You have her eyes and, of course, her coloring."

She smiled. "Some people would agree."

They sat, carefully formal, on either side of the fireplace, making polite inquiries about each other's health and discussing the vagaries of English weather until Rawlings, still bristling with disapproval at such a flagrant breach of etiquette, set a silver tray on the low table between them. Lucy noted, as Rawlings poured out the fragrant China tea, that he had used the best china, the Spode, as if to impose some kind of formality upon the proceedings, of which he clearly took a dim view.

"I hope you find your lodgings at the Golden Lion comfortable," Lucy said.

"Apart from the fact that my head strikes the ceiling every time I stand upright, very comfortable. Those low beams are picturesque but not designed to accommodate any one over five feet tall."

Lucy laughed. "They say that the inn is one of the oldest in the whole of Devonshire. It even has a ghost called the White Maiden." Her tongue was running away with her again, she thought, seeing his mouth crinkle at the corners. "Apparently," she rushed on, "when she was deserted by her lover, she threw herself down the stairs and broke her neck. They say that she is often seen on the landing at midnight."

"Really? Well, I saw no sign of the lady last night, and I doubt if I will ever have the pleasure, as my stay there is shortly to come to an end."

Lucy forced herself to sound unconcerned. "So you are leaving for America quite soon?"

"No. I plan to take a house and spend a few months here in the neighborhood. In fact, I'm going to look over a residence called Ravenscourt Hall this afternoon. It's not far from here. Do you know it?"

She put down her cup carefully and looked at him, trying to keep the sudden joy she was feeling from showing in her face. "Of course I do. It is a wonderful old mansion with a boating lake. I remember going there when I was young. My parents were friends of the people who once owned it."

"You look surprised."

Lucy was now quite unable to meet his eyes. "Lintern Magna is the last place I thought would interest you."

"You are right," he said. "Beautiful as this place is, that is not why I am here. You must know the reason I am. I couldn't stop thinking about you. Believe me, I tried. I told myself that we were from different worlds. That we knew nothing about each other."

"That's true," she murmured.

"But last night, when you looked up and smiled at me, I knew that I had been right to come."

He left his chair and went to her, taking her hands in his. "I tried to write to you so many times, but I couldn't find the words. I kept telling myself that I should forget you and go home. But somehow, I couldn't bring myself to do that without seeing you one more time."

She looked into his eyes, and what she saw there made her tremble with emotion.

"I want to stay here for a while," he said. "So that I can be near you. We can get to know each other better. And then, perhaps, you might begin to believe that you and I were meant for each other."

He lifted a hand to touch her cheek, brushing soft tendrils of hair from her face. She saw a depth of passion in his eyes that made her catch her breath. And then, without any conscious movement by either of them, they were in each other's arms. When their lips met, a flame leaped inside her, and for a few heady moments she seemed to lose awareness of her surroundings.

It was the sudden sound of loud voices in the Great Hall that had them both leaping apart. And, seconds later, the door was flung open, and a burly figure marched into the room, arms outstretched in greeting.

"Lucy, my dear! Home at last!"

"Papa!" Lucy flew across the room into his arms, hiding

her flushed face in the lapels of his riding coat. "I thought you were not returning until next week."

But Guy Ashleigh was staring fiercely over his daughter's head at the stranger standing at the fireplace. He detached himself from Lucy's embrace and strode toward him. "I beg your pardon, sir," he said, his brow furrowing. "I don't believe I have had the pleasure."

"Papa, this is Major Charles Ryman," Lucy said hastily, struggling to appear composed. It was bad enough to have been discovered alone with Charles, but she could not bear to think what her father would have said and done had he come into the room a second or two earlier. "We met in Florence. Major Ryman, this is my father, Sir Guy Ashleigh."

The two men bowed, eyeing each other. "I'm honored to meet you, sir," Charles said. "Your daughter has spoken a great deal about you and your family."

"Indeed?" Guy Ashleigh's eyes were hostile. "Then you have the advantage of me, sir. I do not believe that my daughter has ever mentioned your name to me."

"Papa!" Lucy turned to him, desperately embarrassed by her father's frigid tone. "Major Ryman is a friend of Sofia's cousin Eduardo Ortalli. We were introduced at a soiree at the Castello."

"Ortalli, you say? Well, he's a decent enough fellow." His expression relaxed somewhat. "So what brings you here, Major, may I inquire?"

Charles looked at him steadily. "I came, sir, to renew my acquaintance with your daughter."

"Really? Your accent suggests that you are a long way from home."

"Yes. I am proud to say that I am a citizen of the United States of America. I reside in New York. But I travel a great deal, mainly in Europe."

"I take it, then, that you are no longer on active duty?"

"I resigned my commission with the 7th Cavalry two years ago."

Guy Ashleigh's black eyebrows shot up. "Custer's regiment!"

"Yes, sir."

There was a long silence as the master of the house, clearly impressed, digested this information, and at last, Lucy broke in anxiously.

"Papa, why have you returned early, and where is Mama, and the children?"

"They are returning tomorrow. The weather has been so wretched over the past week—nothing but rain and gales—that we decided it was time to come home. I left early to make certain that everything be made ready for their arrival. I must speak to the servants. There will be much to do."

"In that case, sir, I shall not take up any more of your time," Charles said at once. "I intend to take a house in the neighborhood, as I mean to spend the rest of season here. I very much hope we will meet again in the near future."

"Why not?" Guy Ashleigh nodded, looking, Lucy thought, considerably less hostile than when he had first arrived.

The two men took their leave of each other cordially enough. And as Charles bid her good-bye, their eyes exchanged a message. And Lucy, with her heart beating fast, was quite certain that every time she saw him, she was more in love with him than the time before.

Chapter Nine

I'm sorry," Isabel Hardwicke said, giving Lucy a malicious little smile. "I hadn't realized that my brother hadn't introduced you to his fiancée. James, that was very naughty of you. Come and do the honors at once!"

It was Sunday morning. They had just emerged from church after one of the rector's rambling sermons and were sheltering in the porch from the driving rain. Lucy had been hoping to avoid the inevitable confrontation. If it had not been for the fact that she had promised to ride home in Grace's carriage, she would have managed to slip away with her parents.

As James, looking extremely ill at ease, made the awkward introductions, the two young women took stock of each other. Lady Dorothea was very good-looking, Lucy decided, but she had a sulky mouth, and her manner lacked charm. She was wearing a red and green plaid coat and jacket, currently the height of fashion, which made Lucy's dark blue velvet look positively outmoded.

"And how are you liking Lintern Magna?" she asked Lady Dorothea.

"Well enough, I suppose. Apart from the weather, of course," she answered, looking bored. "I declare, it rains here more in one day than it does in Norfolk in a year!"

Lucy agreed that of late the weather had, indeed, been unusually inclement.

"It almost kept us at home this morning," Isabel said. "And by the empty pews, I see that we were braver than most." She looked at Lucy, her eyes faintly mocking. "We wondered whether Major Ryman might have attended Matins this morning. You and he are well acquainted, are you not, Dorothea?"

"I was introduced to him in Norfolk by my father," Dorothea said, and Lucy was sure she was not imagining the altered note in her voice or the sudden color in her cheeks.

"I really think we ought to leave before the weather gets worse." James, who had been standing there fidgeting, turning the brim of his hat around and around with nervous fingers, suddenly broke in. "The carriage has been waiting long enough." And Lucy, who knew him so well, was certain that he, too, had noticed his fiancée's reaction and wanted the conversation to end.

She and Grace shared an umbrella as they hurried down the path to the lych-gate and collapsed, laughing, inside the barouche, their faces pink with exertion.

And when she got her breath back, Grace was intrigued by Lucy's account of the conversation with Dorothea.

"That's interesting. Tell me, has Major Ryman mentioned her at all?"

"Only that he had met her in Norfolk."

"Then perhaps you imagined that she looked embarrassed," Grace said.

Lucy frowned. "Perhaps. But Isabel wanted me to know that they had met. I could tell by the expression in her eyes."

Grace shook her head. "I shouldn't think that there is anything significant about it. Perhaps there might have been some mild flirtation in the past, but she is James' fiancée now."

"But what if Charles was in love with her? She is beautiful, after all."

"Nonsense. She has a poor complexion, and her eyes are much too small. Also, she is overdressed. That plaid ensemble positively clashed with her red hair."

"That's all superficial. She may have a fascinating personality."

Lucy raised an eyebrow. "Not in my view. Whenever I have been in her company, she has little to say for herself."

But Lucy was not convinced. She was certain that she had

not imagined the expression on Dorothea's face. Perhaps, she thought, when she next saw Charles, she would bring up her name and try to gauge his reaction.

A few days later, an invitation to visit Ravenscourt Hall arrived, and Lucy was barely able to contain her delight. It was to be a luncheon party, and if the weather was kind, it was to be held al fresco, on the terrace.

"Do you think Papa will accept?" she asked, eyeing her stepmother apprehensively. "I believe Lord and Lady Hardwicke have already called upon Major Ryman and intend to join the party. And I know Grace and Philip will be there."

"Of course your papa will accept. We are both looking forward to the occasion."

"May I come too, Mama?" Little Antonia, now fully recovered and apt to follow her older sister wherever she went, fixed her bright eyes upon her mother's face beseechingly. "I can wear my new blue gown and walk about with Lucy and Grace."

Adeline laughed and shook her head. "I'm afraid you must stay at home with your brothers, my love. Children have not been invited." She touched her little daughter's cheek. "I'm sorry if you're disappointed, but I think you would be dreadfully bored."

"I'm not disappointed!" said Piers, who, the image of his father, was happiest out of doors, preferably astride a horse. "I hate going to parties."

"So do I!" Harry, the younger and more studious of the two boys, gave his little sister a stern look as her bottom lip stuck out. "And you're not to be a crybaby. Who wants to spend all afternoon with grown-up people? I don't!"

"Well, I am looking forward to it," his mother said. "A luncheon party out of doors, followed by a walk through the gardens, sounds delightful. Ravenscourt has been shut up ever since the Marchments left for London over a year ago, and it is lovely to think it now has a tenant who will truly appreciate it."

Lucy gazed at Adeline with starry eyes. "You will like

Major Ryman, Mama. I promise you. I so look forward to your meeting him."

"And so do I." But her stepmother's cheerful smile was faintly tinged with disquiet. Lucy had talked of very little else since the family had arrived home, and it was perfectly clear from her flushed cheeks and rapt expression that Lucy was in love.

Her father had taken a dim view of it. "I tell you, Adeline, there the fellow stood in my library, as bold as brass!" he had informed his wife indignantly. "And Lucy looking as if butter wouldn't melt in her mouth!"

His outraged expression had made Adeline smile. "And is Major Ryman as engaging as Lucy has led me to believe?"

"He's a gentleman—I'll give him that. But when all is said and done, the man's a foreigner! What the devil is he doing here, taking a house and calling upon my little girl without a by-your-leave? Tell me that!"

She shook her head. "I'm afraid, my love, you can't blame the poor man for being interested in Lucy," she said. "He is not likely to meet anyone prettier or sweeter-natured. Besides, they probably do things quite differently in America. If he is half as charming and agreeable as she seems to think, she could do a lot worse."

And when, the following week, Charles Ryman welcomed the Ashleighs into his new home, Lady Adeline soon realized that her stepdaughter had not been exaggerating.

It had been some years since Lucy had last visited Ravenscourt Hall. In fact, she had been quite young when she last remembered being there. And when she and her parents arrived at the house at the appointed hour, she found herself viewing it with fresh eyes, eager to inspect the residence Charles had chosen for his stay in Lintern Magna.

The first view of the house was through a narrow gateway with tall stone pillars. Built of silver-gray limestone, with mullioned windows and Dutch gables, its proportions were elegant, intimate, and graceful. It was set in landscaped gardens that sloped gently down to the lake.

On that bright autumn day, with the sun glancing off the surface of the water, the view from the terrace was charming, but Lucy was only aware of Charles Ryman as he came striding across the terrace to greet them.

She could tell immediately by the expression on Adeline's face as he bent over her hand that she was taken with him.

"I hope you are pleased with your new home, Major Ryman," she said. "Next to our own, I think Ravenscourt must be my favorite house in the area."

"It is very pleasant, indeed, and the views are magnificent."

"And do you intend to stay in our neighborhood for long?"

"I"m not sure." He glanced quickly, almost involuntarily, at Lucy. "But at least until Christmas. I have business in London to attend to before returning to America."

"In that case, you'll need to get yourself a decent mount if you intend to come out regularly with the Hunt," Guy Ashleigh informed him. "And, as it happens, I know exactly who can help you."

Lucy watched her father draw Charles into conversation with the Hardwickes and exchanged a relieved glance with her stepmother. It was so important to her that her parents liked him—more important than she had ever thought possible. And there was no reason, she told herself, that they shouldn't. He was handsome, charming, and his manners were impeccable. And he was also an excellent host, careful to divide his time among his guests and making sure that their every need was catered for.

Lunch was served al fresco on the terrace, and Charles had clearly gone to a great deal of trouble with the catering. There was lobster, game pie, pheasant, and pate, accompanied by the finest of wines, followed by jellies and ices. But, delicious as the array of delicacies appeared, his presence robbed her of her appetite. From time to time, their eyes were drawn irresistibly to each other, and she found herself remembering the last time she had eaten out of doors on the day of the picnic at Fiesole. The occasion could not have been more different, and she found herself missing the cheerful informality of the di Lorenzo family gathering. There, Charles Ryman had been accepted into their midst and made welcome. Here, she was aware of the fact that his every word and movement was under scrutiny, and later, when the party was over, he would be the subject of eager debate.

She turned to Grace, who was seated next to her, as they sipped the fragrant Earl Gray tea served at the end of the luncheon. "I wish people would not stare at Charles as if he was some strange being from another world!" she whispered.

"It is only because they find him so fascinating—his accent, of course, and that exotic look about him."

"What does Philip think of him?"

"Oh, you know Philip. A man only has to have a good seat on a horse to impress him."

Lucy heard the faint note of rancor in her friend's voice and looked at her in surprise. It was not like Grace to be spiteful.

"Yes," she went on. "He is still euphoric about the excellent day out they had yesterday. They ran the fox to earth in Breecher's Field after only a three-mile run, and Major Ryman was in at the kill."

"Don't!" Lucy put up a hand in protest. "That's not what I wished to hear."

"Well, I'm sure he has many other good qualities, as well," Grace said hastily. "Shall we walk down to the lake? Everyone seems to be leaving the table." She slipped her arm through Lucy's and drew her away across the terrace. The afternoon sun was unusually hot, and they were forced to put up their parasols as they crossed the lawn until they reached the shade of the pathway that meandered through the trees toward the lake.

"You really are serious about him, aren't you?" Grace had noticed the swift, intimate glance Lucy had exchanged with Charles as she left the table.

"Yes." She glanced at her friend. "Why do you ask?"

"I wondered if he had said anything."

"About?"

"You know perfectly well what I mean!" Grace said impatiently. "Has he made his intentions clear?"

Lucy colored. "Not in so many words. But there has been no opportunity as yet." She examined her friend's face. "Why do you look so doubtful?"

"It's just that you hardly know him."

Lucy frowned. "You forget, Grace, that I spent some time in his company in Italy. And even my father was impressed by his military background. He was decorated, you know, for gallantry."

"But there must also be much that you don't know. For example, if he asked you to marry him, would you be prepared to go with him to live in America?"

Lucy, taken aback, looked away. It was foolish of her, but until this moment she had not seriously considered such a possibility. In her daydreams, she had only imagined sharing her life with Charles here in England. Thoughts of America had not really entered her mind.

"Would you," Grace persisted relentlessly, "be willing to leave your home to live so very far away—and in a country you have never visited?"

There was a long, thoughtful silence. It would be a dreadful wrench to leave her family and friends, and she could not imagine life without them. But if Charles Ryman asked her to be his wife and go with him to New York, would she be able to refuse him?

Lucy shook her head. "It's not something I need to think about yet."

"You see?" Grace said. "You can't answer that question because you're not sure you could be happy with him. And I don't blame you!"

"What are you suggesting?" Lucy was puzzled.

Grace could not quite meet her friend's eye. "It is just that Major Ryman is a complete stranger to us all, and as such, we are forced to take him at face value."

"Grace!" Lucy said. "Look at me! Have you discovered something about Charles that you feel I ought to know?"

Grace shook her head. "It's nothing, just idle speculation. But you are my dearest friend, Lucy, and I want nothing but the best for you."

Lucy was far from satisfied with her answer and would have pressed Grace to say more had they not heard footsteps behind and turned to find Philip and Charles striding toward them.

"We have decided to take you ladies boating!" Philip announced.

"Boating?" Grace stared at her husband in alarm. "Absolutely not! I can't possibly!" Her green moiré dress had an elaborately draped underskirt with flounces and ruffles and was utterly unsuitable for such an activity.

Her husband laughed. "Of course you can!" He took her arm and, ignoring her indignant protests, bore her off toward the boathouse.

Lucy, who was extremely glad that she was wearing her blue velvet day suit, which had no bustle and only a short train, smiled at Charles.

"Poor Grace! She will hate every minute."

"And you?"

Her eyes sparkled. "I'm looking forward to it."

"Good." Charles offered her his arm as they followed the others down the path to the wooden landing stage, where there were several small rowing boats rocking gently in the blue water.

"I'd forgotten about the tiny island," Lucy said, gazing out across the lake. "I remember that it had a folly."

"I'm afraid it's now in ruins."

"How sad. I remember being rowed across there once, when I was young. It was thrilling—a place of enchantment!"

Charles' eyes took hers prisoner. "Perhaps," he said, "we can recapture some of the magic."

He dropped into the boat, bracing himself astride the gunwales as he removed his jacket and laid it on the seat for Lucy to sit on.

When he held out his hand, the boat began to rock alarmingly, and she hesitated. "Trust me," he said. "You'll be quite safe. I promise you a pleasant voyage."

Trust him? As she took his hand and stepped down into the boat, Lucy knew that she would have trusted him with her life.

"Poor Grace!" Lucy turned her head, laughing at Grace's shrieks as her husband bundled her unceremoniously into the other boat and rowed off before she had time to change her mind.

Then, as Charles slipped the oars into the rowlocks and headed across the sparkling water in quite the opposite direction, she stared at him in alarm.

"Where are you taking me?"

"To your enchanted island, of course," he said.

She looked over her shoulder nervously and saw that Philip's boat was rapidly disappearing around a curving bank of the lake. What her father would say if he saw her skimming across the water alone with a man, she would rather not imagine. But then, she turned back and looked at Charles smiling at her, and suddenly she didn't care. She took off her gloves to trail a hand in the water and turned her face up to the sun. What did it matter about one's complexion? It was glorious to feel the warmth of the sunshine on her skin.

"Tell me what you are thinking about," he said.

She smiled at him. This was a moment she would never forget: the gentle movement of the boat, the rhythmic creak of the oars, the dark ripple of the water, even the texture of Charles' coat beneath her fingers, as she glided across the lake like some heroine in an Arthurian legend, with the man of her dreams at the helm.

"I was thinking," she said, "that whatever happens in the future, I shall always have this to remember."

"And I," he said, "was thinking that the future is more important than the past. That it is better to look forward than to look back."

There was something in his voice as she looked across at

him, and for a moment, she thought she saw a shadow cross his face.

But the next moment he was smiling, and she was sure she had imagined it. The boat was nosing into the bank of the tiny island, and through the wild tangle of plants and trees, Lucy could make out the ruined walls of the folly. Charles shipped the oars and allowed the little boat to drift beneath the trailing branches of the weeping willows.

She glanced over her shoulder. They were completely screened from the sight of anyone on the lake or its banks.

"Alone at last," Charles said softly.

Lucy looked at him, and the moment was charged with such breathless excitement, she was unnerved and looked away. "We should go back," she said shakily. "This is really inappropriate."

"I know. But I have been trying hard to observe your absurd English rules of etiquette all week. Which is why I have been obliged to invite a group of strangers to my home in order to spend a few minutes alone with you."

She smiled. "But now that we have accepted your hospitality, you may come and see me as often as you like."

He leaned closer to her, his face half in shadow. "If I had my way, you would never be out of my sight."

They stared at each other in the green darkness under the shadows of the sun-dappled leaves. Suddenly, alone, hidden from curious eyes, the knowledge of their seclusion filled Lucy with delirious excitement.

She watched as Charles tied the mooring rope to the stump of a fallen tree and stepped out beneath the ruined walls of the folly.

He held out his hand, and she took it with barely a moment's hesitation. And as he bent to help her out of the boat, she found herself clasped very firmly in his arms.

"I . . . we really should go," she whispered with a little, trembling laugh.

But Charles went on holding her close. "Suppose," he said, his mouth very close to her cheek, "the boat drifted away.

Suppose we were marooned here, and no one came to find us . . ."

She looked up at him, with her heart fluttering inside her chest like a frightened bird in a cage. "That could never happen."

"I wish it could."

They gazed at each other in the silence. The air under the trees was humid, heady with the scent of meadow sweet and marsh marigold. "We must go back," she murmured. "Everyone will be wondering where we are. Besides, you are neglecting your other guests."

But despite the brave words, she stayed where she was, in the circle of his arms, hardly daring to breathe. She could feel the warmth of his body through his fine cotton shirt, and his breath came sweet and clean against her cheek. Everything she had been taught about decorum and the rules that a properly raised young woman should obey no longer mattered. She was suddenly awakened to the spirit of romance, of recklessness and daring, and slowly, as if she was hypnotized, she raised her head and offered her lips to his.

They kissed with all the pent-up passion and longing of the past weeks they had spent apart, both helpless in the grip of the powerful emotion that had taken them both prisoner. His lips claimed hers again and again, and from deep inside herself came a surge of longing and desire.

It was she who came to her senses first, and she was shaking as she drew away from him.

He caught her hands. "Lucy. Look at me."

She shook her head. "We must go back."

But his hands still clung to hers. "Do you really want to?"

She saw the look of passion in his eyes and drew her hands from his.

"Yes. We must!" She turned away, suddenly shocked at the impropriety of her behavior, horrified at what her parents would say if they found out that she had been alone on the island with Charles—and, worse, that she had behaved like a wanton and allowed such intimacy.

"Please," he said, "wait a moment. I must speak to you . . ."

But Lucy had gained control of her senses and would not look at him. "Please take me back to the boathouse, Charles," she said, and although there was a tremor in her voice, her tone left him in no doubt as to her intentions.

"Of course." Charles stood back, immediately contrite, and as he helped her back into the boat, his manner was carefully formal and correct.

For a few minutes, they remained in silence, and Lucy kept her eyes firmly on the other side of the lake as the boathouse came into view. She had never been kissed like that before. She was in love, and it was wonderful and terrifying and bewildering, and she had no idea what to do about it.

"Forgive me if I have upset you," he said at last.

She shook her head. And still she could not look at him. Her lips still burned from their kisses. How could she accept his apology when she knew she was equally to blame?

As they neared the boathouse, she saw Grace and Philip waiting for them on the landing stage and lifted a hand to wave at them. Had they noticed the sudden disappearance? And, if so, what would they be thinking?

"Lord Hardwicke has invited me to dine tomorrow," Charles said, forcing her to turn to her head. "I believe you will be there too."

"Yes," she said repressively, "with my parents. And perhaps"—she glanced at him quickly—"James and Lady Dorothea."

But Charles' face remained impassive as he nosed the boat into its mooring.

"Until tomorrow, then?"

Lucy did not reply, but as he helped her out of the boat, she knew that the hours ahead, as she waited to see him again, would seem like years.

Chapter Ten

Lucy had no opportunity to speak to Grace privately for the rest of the day. But the expression in her friend's eyes told her everything she needed to know. Her aberrant behavior had been noticed, and Grace was clearly concerned.

Grace was her dearest friend, Lucy thought on the way home in the carriage, but as an older, married woman, there were times when her sense of propriety seemed rather excessive. Her unspoken disapproval changed Lucy's sense of shame to sudden defiance. What if she had been alone with Charles? It was important to move with the times, after all! And although the rules of society were strict, there were signs that they were becoming less rigid. Only the other day, she had been reading in the *Times* about the so-called "new women" who went about unchaperoned and were not afraid to speak up for themselves in male company.

Not that Grace would approve of such behavior! Unlike Cousin Sofia, who had encouraged her friendship with Charles Ryman, Grace had made it clear that she had reservations about him, without actually saying why. Lucy hoped there would be a chance to speak to her about it when they dined with her parents the following evening.

It was a great relief to discover that her adventure on the lake had otherwise gone unnoticed. Her parents both seemed to approve of Charles. They had thoroughly enjoyed their day, and they seemed genuinely pleased that he had been invited to join them at the Hardwickes.

Lucy spent the whole day in anticipation of the event. Normally, she found dinner parties rather dull, but she could hardly restrain her excitement at the thought of the unexpected extra guest. She was dressed and ready to depart an hour before it was necessary, and the care she had taken with her appearance was rewarded by the admiration of her small sister when she went to her bedroom to say good night.

"Oh, Lucy, you look so lovely! I wish I could put flowers in my hair and wear a beautiful dress and go to dinner with grown-up people!"

"That will happen quite soon enough," her mother said, smiling as she kissed Antonia good night.

Lucy had chosen a chiffon gown of the palest blue with a small bustle and a high neckline edged with Venice lace. The silver beading on the close-fitting bodice and hem emphasized her tiny waist and sparkled with her every movement. Her skin glowed, and her eyes shone, and there was an aura about her that was unmistakable. Lucy was in love.

She turned to her stepmother with a shy smile.

"Will I do?"

"My dearest girl, I have never seen you look lovelier."

"Ladies!" Guy Ashleigh's voice rang out. His patience was wearing thin as he paced about at the foot of the staircase. "Am I to wait all evening? The carriage is here, and we shall be late!"

And, smiling at each other conspiratorially, his wife and daughter hurried downstairs to join him.

When the Ashleighs walked into the white-and-gold drawing room at Hardwicke House, they found that the other guests had already arrived.

"Here we are! A thousand apologies for our late arrival." Guy Ashleigh bent over his hostess' hand. He threw a mischievous glance at his wife and daughter. "I will never understand why ladies take so long to dress. I swear, they kept me waiting for half an hour."

As his wife shot him a reproving look, Lady Hardwicke laughed. "Nonsense, Guy, I don't believe a word of it. Besides, you are not late. We are not dining until seven."

Lucy had seen Charles immediately as she walked into the room. He was deep in conversation with Lord Hardwicke and Philip. But her pleasure, when he looked up to smile at her, was tempered by the sight of George and Isabel Hardwicke. For some reason, she had not expected them to be present. Still, she thought, there was no sign of James and his fiancée, and Grace was here. That was a comfort.

"Come and sit down." Lady Hardwicke drew Lucy and her stepmother toward the rest of the group. "There is no need for introductions. I believe everyone has met Major Ryman. In fact, Lucy, I understand that we are indebted to you for making his acquaintance."

"Yes." Lucy willed herself not to appear flustered. "We met in Florence."

"And was it your first visit to Italy, Major Ryman?"

"By no means," Charles said. "I have traveled there a great deal on business. Have you ever visited Florence, Lady Hardwicke?"

"No. But my daughter-in-law has. You were extremely impressed by the architecture, were you not, Isabel?"

"Oh, indeed! But, of course, Rome is far superior to Florence in every way."

As Isabel took center stage to extol the glories of the Eternal City, Lucy exchanged significant glances with her stepmother. Isabel had never made a secret of her hostility toward Adeline, even before the unfortunate affair between Lucy and her youngest brother, James, and in company they had little to say to each other.

The reason for their mutual aversion to each other had always puzzled Lucy until Grace had thrown some light on the situation. "From what Mama has told me, Isabel was once in love with your father. Everyone expected them to marry, but he chose your stepmother instead."

Lucy quite understood why. Isabel was elegant, of course, and considered to be extremely fashionable, but she couldn't hold a candle to Adeline, either in looks or in nature.

As soon as she was able to, Lucy slipped away from the

animated group, which was now vigorously disputing the merits of various Italian cities, and joined Grace on the sofa.

"Isabel always has to be the center of attention," Grace whispered behind her fan. "If I'd known she was going to be here, I would have made Philip come without me."

"I'm glad you didn't."

Grace looked at her penetratingly. "I am dying to know what happened to you yesterday."

Lucy, conscious of Charles' eyes upon her, frowned, shaking her head. "Later."

"That hateful boat ride!" Grace whispered. "Philip can be so annoying! My gown was ruined, and he thought it was very amusing! But you," she added accusingly, "looked as if you were enjoying every minute!"

Lucy was saved by the arrival of the Hardwickes' butler.

"Dinner is served, my lady."

"Thank you, Palmer." Lady Hardwicke turned to her guests with a smile. "Shall we go in?"

Lucy looked cool and composed as Charles came to offer her his arm, but as he escorted her to the dining room, the hand resting on his sleeve was trembling.

As they walked slowly down the long corridor, she was acutely aware of the fact that George and Isabel were walking close behind them. She could almost feel the cold green eyes boring into her back, and she was certain she could hear Isabel whispering.

But Charles seemed totally oblivious to everyone except Lucy. "Have you forgiven me yet for my behavior yesterday?" he asked her, with a rueful lift of one eyebrow.

She would not risk a glance at him. "There is nothing to forgive, since I was equally to blame."

"That is not entirely true. But thank you." His arm pressed her hand against him. "I have to go to London tomorrow on business. May I see you when I get back? Perhaps you would let me take you for a drive."

She shook her head. Did he know nothing about English

etiquette? She could not possibly ride about the country in a carriage without a chaperone. Her father would not hear of it.

"Then I will call."

She nodded and allowed him to seat her next to him. The long, mahogany table was set with bowls of fresh flowers, and the silverware and crystal gleamed softly in the candlelight.

With Charles on her left and Philip on her right, Lucy would have felt relaxed and happy among friends and family had it not been for the hard, cold stare of Isabel Hardwicke directly opposite. Try as Lucy would to join in the laughter and chatter, her eyes returned to Isabel again and again. It might have been a flight of fancy, but it seemed to Lucy that there was a watchfulness about her, an air of anticipation, as if, like some sleek predator, she was waiting for the chance to pounce.

"I hope you enjoy curried meat, Major Ryman," boomed Lord Hardwicke as the footmen stepped forward to remove the soup plates from the first course, a truly delicious beef consommé.

"I must confess, sir, it is a dish I have never tasted."

"Really? Then I do hope the flavor will not be too pungent for you," Lady Hardwicke said. "We have become rather fond of spicy dishes. Our cook has always liked to serve traditional English food, but now that Mrs. Beeton herself has included some curry recipes in her new cookery book, Cook has become quite adventurous."

Every eye was fixed upon Charles as he sampled the hot, aromatic flavor of lamb stewed with hot chilli peppers and exotic Indian spices, and when he pronounced it delicious, there was a ripple of applause.

Only Isabel Hardwicke refrained from joining in. Instead, she fixed her icy gaze upon Charles' face, her eyes glittering with malice.

"I am surprised," she said, "that you have never eaten a dish of curry before, Major Ryman. My brother's fiancée, Lady Dorothea Fitzallan, tells me that you often dined at Fitzallan House. And, of course, their chef is renowned for his Indian cuisine."

Charles put down his fork and looked across the table, his face expressionless. "On the few occasions on which I dined with the Earl," he said, "we enjoyed game from his estate in Norfolk."

"He has one of the finest hunting lodges in the county," George said. "Second only, of course, to the Prince of Wales' estate at Sandringham."

"So I've heard," said Guy Ashleigh. "Fitzallan has a reputation as a keen sportsman."

Philip nodded. "I was told that, last season, his guests shot almost three thousand pheasants in a single day."

"How horrible!" Lucy made a face. "Poor birds. I think it is such a cruel, unnecessary sport, don't you, Grace?"

"Yes, absolutely!"

"Nonsense!" Philip laughed at his wife's expression. "I didn't notice you turn up your nose when we were served grouse at the Wyatts' the other day!"

Grace made a face. "If you must know, I thought it impolite to refuse."

"James would have been disappointed if you had. He brought back a dozen brace from Norfolk last week."

"The boy is a first-class shot, I'll give him that," said Lord Hardwicke. "He and his prospective father-in-law will have a great deal in common."

"Absolutely," said George with an awkward look at Lucy.

Lucy was perfectly aware that at the mention of the name, an atmosphere had been created, and she was at its center. If only, she thought with irritation, people would stop linking her with James and realize that she was no longer remotely interested in him.

Her parents were watching her anxiously, and at the end of the table, Grace, looking indignant, was trying to catch her eye.

Isabel's chiseled lips curved into an ironic little smile.

"Have you met my brother, Major Ryman?" Isabel was clearly determined to make the most of the situation. "I merely ask because you and his fiancée are such old friends."

There was a faint streak of color across Charles Ryman's cheekbones as he raised his head to look directly at Isabel.

"No, I'm afraid I have not had the pleasure."

"Really? Then we must introduce you as soon as possible." She allowed her eyes to rest very briefly upon Lucy. "I'm certain you will have a great deal in common. You seem to have such similar tastes. Don't you agree, Miss Ashleigh?"

A wave of color flooded Lucy's face. She stared across the table and made no reply.

George, embarrassed by his wife's remarks, rushed to the rescue. "James will almost certainly be here at the Hunt on Wednesday. Will you be joining us, Major?"

"I'm afraid not." His voice, though cold, was perfectly polite. "I have business in London to attend to and will be away for a few days."

Lady Hardwicke, aware of the sudden tension, was determined to steer the conversation into safer waters. "You seem so much at home in our country, Major Ryman. Am I correct in assuming your family is of English extraction?"

"My grandfather was born in London. He visited New York as a young man, met and married my grandmother, and decided to remain there. He became naturalized, took American citizenship, and then went on to become a successful businessman."

"But how very romantic! He must," observed Lady Ashleigh, "have been very much in love, to leave his home and family."

"Yes, I believe he was," Charles said quietly. "Their marriage was very happy, and he never regretted it."

And, although he never looked in Lucy's direction, she somehow felt that his words were meant for her.

Lucy had been dreading the moment when the ladies retired to leave the gentlemen to their port and cigars. The thought of dealing with the sarcastic tongue of Isabel Hardwicke was daunting. But she need not have worried. As they rose from the table, Isabel complained of a headache and asked for her carriage to be brought round. And the minute she left, the atmosphere lifted.

"Poor Isabel," Lady Hardwicke said. "George tells me that she suffers dreadfully with migraine. She should probably not have come this evening, but when she heard that we were entertaining Major Ryman, she insisted upon it."

I'm sure she did, Lucy thought, exchanging a discreet but meaningful glance with Grace.

Without her caustic presence, soon the ladies were deep in happy conversation about the latest neighborhood happenings.

As the others discussed the arrangements for the annual Harvest Supper, Lucy felt her mind wandering. It had not been easy, listening to the exchanges between Charles and Isabel at the dinner table. Her references to Lady Dorothea had been deliberately provocative and had seemed to hint at some kind of hidden significance. Charles' reaction, too, troubled Lucy. He had looked defensive and uncomfortable, and once again Lucy found herself remembering that brief encounter with Dorothea at the Hunt Ball.

It was galling to realize that Isabel Hardwicke had, after all, achieved her purpose, for when the gentlemen joined them in the drawing room, Lucy felt unaccountably angry with Charles and did not look directly at him when he walked into the room.

"Shall I tell Palmer to bring in the card table, my dear?" Lord Hardwicke asked his wife.

"Why not? I realize we are an odd number, but we could play at knockout whist if everyone is agreeable."

"Capital idea," Guy Ashleigh said, turning to Charles. "What do you say? Or is whist too tame for you?"

Lord Hardwicke gave one of his booming laughs. "I imagine you're a poker player, Major!" He clapped him on the shoulder jovially. "I'll wager it wouldn't be an easy task to read your mind!"

Charles gave a brief smile, which never reached his eyes. "I'm afraid I don't play cards at all," he said, his voice very cool and controlled. "But you mustn't let that spoil everyone else's enjoyment. If you will excuse me, I'll bid you all good night. I have business in London tomorrow and must rise early." He turned to Lady Hardwicke and bowed over her hand. "Please accept my thanks for your hospitality, your ladyship. It has been a delightful evening."

And with a bow and a smile to the assembled company, he turned and left the room.

The silence, when the door closed behind him, was palpable. Lucy sat as if carved from stone, utterly bewildered by the sudden exit, and it was Lady Hardwicke who spoke first.

"How extraordinary!" She gave her husband a rueful smile. "I'm afraid our guests seem to be disappearing at an alarming rate tonight, my love! I hope no one else is about to follow suit."

During the hasty chorus of denials that ensued, Lucy tried to gather her thoughts. What had possessed Charles to make such a hasty and ill-judged exit? He must surely have realized that it might give offense.

Her father gave voice to her unspoken questions. "What the devil has gotten into the fellow?" he demanded. "When we mentioned playing cards, it was as if we were asking him to commit a crime."

"Perhaps," Lady Hardwicke said, "it goes against his religious beliefs. Some people, you know, feel that it is sinful. I have heard playing cards referred to as the devil's pictures."

George laughed. "I don't think, Mama, that anyone would object to an innocent game of whist played in a lady's drawing room. Even the rector joins in when he comes to dine."

Adeline Ashleigh glanced at her stepdaughter's set face sympathetically.

"Perhaps," she said, "the card game had nothing to do with Major Ryman's reasons for leaving. After all, he has a long journey to make tomorrow, and it is quite late."

"That's true," Philip said.

George shook his head. "Mark my words, there's more to it than that."

"My guess is," Lord Hardwicke said, "that the fellow's a gambler. He had a distinctly odd expression on his face when

I mentioned poker. They say there's a gambling saloon in every town in America."

"I think you may have something there, sir. He is an agreeable chap and excellent company. But," George added, "from what my wife tells me, our Major Ryman is something of a dark horse."

"In what respect?" Guy Ashleigh demanded.

Lucy, with her cheeks flaming, looked across at George angrily. Suddenly, she couldn't bear listening to this discussion any longer. But even as she put away her stepmother's gently restraining hand and opened her mouth to protest, Lady Hardwicke forestalled her.

"I really don't think, gentlemen, that this is the kind of conversation that should be conducted in the drawing room. Now, may I suggest that we play cards and enjoy the rest of the evening?"

"Of course, Mama." And George, looking rather sheepish, went to the cabinet to fetch the cards.

In deference to her ladyship's wishes, Lucy, who longed to go home, forced herself to join in and disguise her feelings. And the rest of the evening passed pleasantly and without incident.

But when she and her parents set off home for the Manor, she sat, silent and disconsolate, in her corner of the coach and stared miserably out the window. The rain, which had set in earlier, and the impenetrable darkness of the countryside only added to her misery. What had George Hardwicke meant, she asked herself, by saying that Charles was a dark horse? And was Lord Hardwicke right in thinking that he was a gambler? Her image of the man she loved was suddenly tarnished, and she wished she had never been invited to the dinner party. At least she would have been spared hearing such unpalatable remarks.

"Why so miserable, Lucy?" Her father, never one to beat about the bush, had noticed his daughter's mood.

Lucy bridled at his words. "I am not miserable, Papa." Then, in a sudden rush of blood to her head, she added, "If I am upset, it is because of the unkind remarks made about Major Ryman."

"Unkind, were they?"

"I think so, yes. And it hurt me to hear a friend spoken of in that way when he was not there to defend himself!"

"Indeed? Well, let me tell you that if I discover that what was said is correct, your friendship is shortly to come to an end."

Lucy's face went hot. "And if it is not correct?"

"That remains to be seen. I shall make the relevant inquiries, and until I am perfectly satisfied that Major Ryman is a man of unimpeachable character, I'm afraid that you will have nothing further to do with him. Is that clearly understood?"

"But, Papa, how can you listen to idle gossip?" Lucy raged. "It's so unfair!"

"That is enough." His voice was implacable. "The subject is closed, and I will not hear another word upon it."

And Lucy, hearing the uncompromising tone of her father's voice, said no more until they arrived home, although her heart felt as if it were bursting. With a muttered "Good night," she marched straight upstairs. And Adeline, exchanging a meaningful glance with her husband, followed her stepdaughter to her room.

She found her sitting at her dressing table in a state of angry distress.

"They said he was a dark horse!" Lucy, having dismissed her maid, sat staring at her own flushed face in the mirror. "What did they mean? What do they think he has done?"

"My poor love!" Adeline went to her and gently began to remove her hairpins to brush out the fall of shining tresses. "You must not upset yourself like this. What was said was mere speculation. But Major Ryman is a stranger. We know nothing about him. You cannot blame your father for being wary. You are so very precious to him."

"I don't care what Papa thinks! He can't stop me from seeing Charles!"

Adeline sighed. "You must be guided by your father, Lucy.

You know how fair-minded he is. He will not be swayed by idle gossip." She dropped a kiss on top of her head. "I'm sure everything will turn out for the best."

But Lucy, still furiously angry and hurt, would not be comforted. When her stepmother had left her room, she lay awake in the darkness until at last she came to the realization that her anger was not so much directed at her father but at Charles. It was hard to admit, but she was very afraid that the comments about him might be true. Her idol might, after all, have feet of clay.

Chapter Eleven

Charles set out for London with a heavy heart, cursing himself for the way in which he had conducted himself at Hardwicke House the previous evening. Even the ever-changing vista offered by the speed of the train as he traveled through the green English countryside failed to interest him. Over and over again, he remembered the look of bewilderment on Lucy's face as he had turned to leave the room. What must they all have thought of such ill-mannered and graceless behavior! He found himself considering writing a note of apology to the Hardwickes. But, on reflection, he decided against the idea. He could not be truthful with them until he had spoken to Lucy, and so the subject was best left; he had no desire to draw any further attention to himself.

Isabel Hardwicke's remarks about Lady Dorothea had been enough of an embarrassment, and he was surprised that Lady Dorothea had confided so readily in her sister-in-law-to-be. He had no doubt that the details of his association with Lord Fitzallan's daughter would soon be the subject of gossip and speculation. It was obvious by the expression on Lucy's face that she had taken note of the comments, and there would come a time when he would need to explain himself to her. In the meantime, he had other pressing matters to worry about.

All in all, it was a tiring journey, and darkness had fallen by the time he reached his club in Piccadilly, where he stayed when he was in London.

As he walked into the paneled hall, with its atmosphere of restrained elegance, he found the familiar surroundings strangely comforting.

"Good evening, Taylor."

"Good evening, Major. May I say how pleasant it is to see you again?" The elderly, silver-haired steward behind the high mahogany desk smiled at him. "Your usual room, sir, I take it? And may I ask whether you are dining this evening?"

"Yes." Charles glanced at his pocket watch, surprised to discover that he was hungry. "I'll need a table in about half an hour."

"Very good, sir. Oh, bear with me for a moment." The steward reached into a pigeonhole behind the desk as Charles was about to turn away. "There are some letters for you."

"Thanks." Charles leafed through the pile quickly and then stopped as his eye fell on an envelope addressed to him in an elegant, feminine hand. A few months ago, he would have been delighted at the sight of it and eager to scan the contents. But now, he felt nothing but a sudden surge of anxiety as he followed the porter to his room on the first floor.

"Can I be of any further assistance, sir?"

Charles tossed him a shilling. "That will be all, thanks."

"Thank *you*, sir!"

When the porter had disappeared with a grin commensurate with the size of the gratuity, Charles tossed the rest of his mail onto the walnut table in the window recess, sat down, and tore open the square white envelope.

The letter had been written several weeks earlier and had reached London only a few days ago. It had clearly been sent to London in the hope of finding him at his club and required no reply. But when he had finished reading the contents, he knew that his fate was sealed. If he wished to achieve his heart's desire and ask Lucy Ashleigh to marry him, he could waste no more time. He must make a clean breast of things and throw himself on her mercy. If only, he thought, he had been frank and open with her from the beginning. Now, he could only hope that she would understand his reluctance to confide in her. And if, as he feared, she would be unable to accept the truth, it was best to know once and for all where he stood.

"You promised," Antonia said, fixing her stepsister with a determined stare. "You promised you would take me to Miss March's! Papa gave me a whole shilling for practicing on the pianoforte for half an hour every day last week, and Mama said I could buy some new clothes for Jane."

Lucy sighed. Jane, currently her sister's favorite doll, had been given to her on her birthday, and she had been longing to visit the emporium where Miss March was renowned for making tiny, exquisite clothing for dolls.

"Yes, I did promise. But Mama thinks the weather is too bad for you to walk as far as the village. And this morning, she needed the carriage to visit Aunt Emma in Exeter."

Since the child's illness, her parents were very careful about her health, and Antonia, naturally, found their concern irksome.

"But it's fine today!" she pleaded. "The rain has quite gone. Please, Lucy! Miss March makes such lovely things for dolls, and Jane needs a new cloak and bonnet."

Lucy looked at the small, woebegone face. Antonia was bored and restless. She missed her brothers very much, and they would not be returning from school until a few days before Christmas. Her new governess was not due to arrive until the New Year, and there was little for her to do.

"What if I put on my warmest cloak and go to Miss March's myself? She will probably let me bring you a selection to choose from, and we can take back what you don't want another day."

Antonia, in transports of delight, flung herself on her sister. "Oh, dearest Lucy, thank you!"

It was the last thing Lucy wanted to do. She had kept herself to herself since the Hardwickes' dinner party. With Charles in London, it was as if the world around her had been robbed of color. Even the weather had been in tune with her dismal mood, and she both longed for and dreaded his return. What if she discovered that George's opinion of him was true? What if her father turned him away if he called at the house? When would she be able to see him again? Her mind was filled with anxious thoughts.

But despite her reluctance to leave the house, the walk to the village proved invigorating. A pale sun flickered through breaks in the scudding clouds, and the wind blew cold and pure off the high moors. As she crossed the bridge, Lucy clung to her bonnet in case it blew off over the parapet. In summer, the Lintern was little more than a lazy stream. Today, it was in full spate after almost a week of heavy rain.

Miss March was horrified to learn that Lucy had walked all the way from the Manor. Her myopic brown eyes behind the steel-framed pince-nez were filled with alarm.

"Miss Ashleigh, do please let me send for the dogcart to take you home," she begged as she wrapped up a bundle of carefully selected doll's clothes. "There is more rain promised, and I am afraid that you will catch your death of cold!"

Lucy smiled. "Thank you, Miss March, for your concern. But I'm sure I shall get home before the next shower."

As it happened, she had hardly reached the end of the street when the skies suddenly opened, and the rain began to pour down relentlessly. Quickly, she stepped into the entrance of the post office to take shelter, the door swung open, and she almost collided with a tall figure.

They stopped short inches away from each other, and Lucy felt her heart turn over.

"Charles!"

His eyes lit up at the sight of her. "I was just thinking about you." He took off his hat. "In fact, I was planning to call at the Manor this afternoon."

"Really?" Lucy's pleasure at the sight of him was quickly tempered by the thought of the reception he would receive. How could she tell him that he would not be welcome at her home? That her father had expressly forbidden her to see him until he learned more of his particulars?

He was looking at her quizzically, as if he caught the uncertain note in her voice.

"I was hoping to see you alone," he said. And then, noticing her wet cloak and bonnet, he moved away from the door. "I'm sorry. Were you about to go inside?"

"No. I was on my way home. I just stopped for a moment to shelter. I've been to Miss March's to buy doll's clothes, of all things." She looked down ruefully at her mud-spattered ankle boots. "It was foolish of me to walk, I suppose. But Mama had taken the carriage, and I felt sorry for poor Antonia. She is not allowed to go out in this weather."

"Then let me drive you home." He pointed to the chaise across the street. "I think we are in for a heavy downpour."

If he noticed her hesitation, he gave no sign of it. He took her arm to cross the street and helped her into the carriage.

"You look anxious," he said, as he got in beside her.

"No." She shook her head quickly. "Just a little tired."

"Are you sure?" He laid his hand over hers, and her heart leaped.

"Yes. Yes, of course." She forced a smile. "It's quite a walk, you know. More than two miles."

He withdrew his hand, and for a few minutes there was an awkward silence, with only the sound of the rain pattering on the windows.

"I haven't seen you since we dined at the Hardwickes'," Lucy said at last. "I hope your visit to London went well?"

"Yes. Very well. I arrived back late last night."

"I suppose," she said, "Lintern Magna must seem very dull in comparison with London."

He shook his head. "Not at all. I love the English countryside. It's beautiful and tranquil. A man could find peace here."

The church clock in the village struck eleven, and the chimes, borne on the wind, carried to them across the river.

"And so you like our way of life?"

"I do. It suits me very well. But I have a business to take care of, and I can't do that away from cities."

She glanced at him quickly. "I haven't seen very much of the world," she said diffidently. "I've been to London, of course, and it did seem very exciting. And I've traveled through Europe. I loved Florence."

"You would like New York. It is a wonderful city, full of contrasts—almost a country in itself. And I have a place in the foothills of the Adirondacks where I was born and raised. It's beautiful there, wild and rugged, a land of lakes and rivers and high peaks. I wish you could see it."

Lucy looked at him, and what she saw in his eyes made her breathless. She turned away quickly. "You must miss being there."

"Sometimes. And however far I travel, I've always been happy to return home." He turned to look directly at her. "Until now."

They stared at each other, and Lucy felt herself trembling with emotion. "But you will still have to go."

She wanted him to say, "No. I will stay here with you forever."

But instead he took her face between his hands. "Yes," he said softly. "I must go. But I hate the thought of it. And you know why."

A sudden squall of wind drove the rain hard against the windows, enclosing them in the dark intimacy of the carriage, and the world outside suddenly retreated. She looked at him, and suddenly they were in each other's arms. They clung to each other, suddenly impervious to the possibility of prying eyes.

He bent his head and kissed her, and at the touch of his lips, a melting sweetness flowed through her body, and she gave herself up to the rapture of the moment.

When he raised his head, her eyes were still closed, her lips parted, and her breath came sweetly through them.

"When do you mean to go?" she asked him, and the words caught in her throat.

"I'm not sure yet." He touched her flushed cheek gently, then tilted her chin so that he could look into her eyes. "I told you once before," he said, "that it depends on you. You see, I have been hoping that my life will change for the better, but I can't tell you about it yet."

"Charles . . ."

He caught her hands and held them against his chest. "Don't say anything. There are things that I need to tell you about myself. Things that might make a difference to the way you feel."

She looked at him, and the expression in his eyes made her suddenly afraid. What did he have to tell her that so troubled him? And suddenly she was remembering the words George Hardwicke had used the other night. *A dark horse.* A man with something to hide.

The carriage slowed and swayed as the horses turned into the Manor gates.

"Tell me!" Lucy said, her dark eyes huge with anxiety. "Tell me now!"

They were speeding up the long, tree-lined drive, and soon their conversation would have to come to an end.

He shook his head. "I need to talk to you at greater length. Come for a drive with me tomorrow."

Lucy looked anxious. She had already crossed the line of propriety by accepting his offer to drive her home. Even with the rain as an excuse, she should not have been alone with him in a closed carriage without a chaperone. "You know that's impossible. My father would never allow it."

She turned as the groom opened the carriage door to help her alight, and Charles stepped down beside her.

"Then, when will I see you again?"

It had stopped raining, and a sudden shaft of sunlight penetrated the clouds. And as she was about to frame an answer, she heard the sound of a horse's hooves along the drive.

"If you wish to hunt tomorrow," she said hastily, casting an agonized glance at the rider advancing toward them at a brisk trot, "the Hunt takes place here."

"And you'll be riding?"

"Yes."

The next minute, the horse was reined in, and Guy Ashleigh dropped from the saddle.

He gave them a look that was distinctly lacking in cordiality.

"Major!" he barked, with a curt nod of the head by way of greeting. Then he turned to his daughter. "What's this, Lucy? Where have you been?"

"Papa!" Lucy said, blushing at his tone. "I walked to the village and was caught in the rain. Major Ryman kindly offered to drive me home."

Her father was clearly not impressed. "I am grateful to you, sir," he said coldly. "Please accept my thanks."

"Not at all. I was happy to have been of assistance." Charles' tone was perfectly polite, but Lucy saw by the look in his eyes that her father's hostility had not gone unnoticed.

"How fortunate," Guy said, with icy deliberation, "that you happened to meet. Although what possessed you, Lucy, to have walked to the village in this weather is beyond my understanding."

"I suppose it was foolish. But Antonia so hates being confined to the house, and I went to buy something to amuse her."

Guy scowled. "She is spoiled enough already." Then, immediately relenting when he saw the hurt expression on his daughter's face, he added, "But it was kind of you to go to so much trouble." He threw a casual glance in Charles' direction. "My daughter's heart often rules her head, Major Ryman. Sometimes that allows people to take advantage of her."

Charles returned his glance gravely. "I can assure you, sir, that I have far too much respect for Miss Ashleigh ever to be guilty of that."

"I'm glad to hear it."

Lucy waited for her father, normally the soul of hospitality, to invite Charles into the house and offer him some refreshment. But he went on standing there, hands clasped behind his back, and said nothing.

Charles touched his hat. "Good day, then, to you both," he said, and he took his leave without ceremony.

Father and daughter watched as the carriage headed back along the drive.

"He's a strange one," Guy Ashleigh said. "I don't know what to make of the fellow."

"Don't you. Papa?" Lucy said bleakly. Not so very long ago she would have trusted her father's judgment above all others'. But now she desperately wanted to believe that it was flawed.

"No. There is something about the man that I cannot quite fathom. And I must tell you, Lucy, that there are rumors circulating about him that I cannot afford to ignore."

Lucy looked at her father mutinously. "It's only because he's not English. People around here know nothing about him, and so they make up stories. Just because he's different, they turn him into a villain."

Her father frowned. "Is that what you think? Well, perhaps you have a point. But until such time that I have grounds to trust the man, I do not wish you to encourage his friendship. Is that clearly understood?"

"Yes, Papa." Lucy said. But as she walked into the house, waves of resentment flooded through her. She loved her father more than life itself, but she was twenty years of age and was tired of being treated like a child. It was high time, she thought defiantly, that she had a life of her own.

Chapter Twelve

Lucy stood in front of the cheval mirror in her room and inspected her appearance. It was months since she had hunted, and she was pleased to see that her riding habit still fitted her like a glove.

The fine cloth of her long black skirt draped elegantly, and the tight-waisted bodice with its long basque and peplum emphasized the curves of her slim figure. On her head she wore a black velvet hat with an ostrich feather, and her gauntlets were of supple leather.

She would not have chosen to hunt that morning. Riding, of course, was a pleasure and always had been ever since her tenth birthday, when her father had presented her with her first pony. But she derived no enjoyment from the thrill of the chase. From her first ride to hounds, when she had been blooded at the age of fifteen, she had been desperately sorry for the plight of the poor, hunted creature and utterly revolted by the proceedings that followed the kill. But today was different. Today, Charles would be there, and her heart beat fast at the thought of seeing him.

Traditionally, on the first Saturday of each month, the Meet took place at the Manor, and Lucy could hear the sound of clattering hooves in the courtyard below mingled with laughter and chatter. When she went to the window and saw the Master in his scarlet coat riding up the drive with his pack of hounds, she hurried downstairs to join her father. Stirrup cup in hand, he was already mounted on Trojan, his huge black hunter. It was an early Meet—only seven o'clock on a sunny autumn morning—and her stepmother, brothers, and sister were still fast asleep on the other side of the house.

As she joined the throng of riders milling around in the courtyard, she was rewarded by her father's smile as he watched a stable lad help her mount Pheasant, her favorite mare, and settle her into the sidesaddle.

"This is an unexpected pleasure, my dear!"

Lucy blushed as she returned his greeting. If he had known exactly why she had decided to join him, she thought ruefully, he might not have been so pleased. He turned to greet Isabel Hardwicke with Dorothea Fitzallan at her side and signalled Lucy to join them.

Isabel was as elegant as ever in a dark green riding habit, but Lucy could not help noticing with a certain degree of satisfaction that the fitted bodice of Dorothea's red-and-cream riding jacket strained a little over her ample bosom and clashed with her hair. Her eyes met Lucy's with a coldly assessing stare, and then Isabel turned and gave a mocking smile.

"My dear Lucy! It must be months since you last hunted! Pray, why have we been accorded such an honor?"

"She likes to please her father," Guy Ashleigh said. "Isn't that so, my dear?"

Lucy tried not to look guilty. "Of course, Papa."

"Where are your menfolk this morning?" Guy demanded. "It's not like them to miss a Hunt."

"George has gone to Exeter to a livestock auction and has taken James with him," Isabel said, and then she gave a sudden, dramatic start. "I'm so sorry! I am forgetting my manners! Dorothea, have you met Guy Ashleigh?"

"No," Dorothea said. "I have not yet had the pleasure. But, of course," she added, with a patronizing smile, "James has told me all about you and your interesting family."

"How d'you do?" The barb quite clearly missed its mark as far as Guy Ashleigh was concerned, and he was already turning away to speak to a neighbor.

But although it was not lost on Lucy, she managed to remain

expressionless. If Dorothea thought that she had scored some kind of victory over her, she was wrong. She would not, she thought, have changed places with her for the whole wide world!

"I hear you have been in Italy, Miss Ashleigh," Dorothea said. "They tell me the heat can be quite suffocating in the summer months."

"Personally, I found the sunshine very pleasant. And Florence is such a beautiful city," Lucy said equably. And then, quite unable to resist, she added, "It was where I met Charles Ryman, you know."

The reaction was instant. The color spread up Dorothea's neck until it stained her cheeks. "He is . . . was a friend of my father's," she muttered.

The next minute, she had turned away to speak to a friend of Isabel's, but too late to disguise her reaction to the mention of Charles.

Lucy stared at her retreating back. So there *was* a connection between them, something that made her distinctly uneasy. Charles had said that he wanted to tell her something about himself, something that might alter her feelings toward him. Was it possible that it might be about Dorothea?

As she mingled with the others, her eyes returned again and again to the long, tree-lined drive, hoping to see Charles Ryman's familiar figure riding toward the house. But as yet there was no sign of him, and as the minutes ticked by and he did not appear, she began to think he had decided not to join them.

Her hopes were fading as the Master gave the signal to move off. But then, just as the Huntsman rallied the yelping hounds with his horn, there was a stir as Charles cantered into the courtyard astride a handsome gray. He was wearing hunting scarlet with immaculate white breeches and gleaming boots, and as he doffed his velvet cap to the Master and threaded his way through the riders toward Guy Ashleigh and his daughter, he drew the attention of the entire gathering.

Lucy saw Isabel Hardwicke turn her head to look at him, noticed her hostile expression, and saw her lean across to say something to Lady Dorothea.

"Good morning." Charles seemed oblivious to their stares. His greeting included both the Ashleighs, but his eyes belonged to Lucy. Painfully aware of her father's watchful presence, she managed a smile that concealed the turmoil inside her.

"Welcome!" The Squire's tone, Lucy noted, was genial enough, and the trio moved off together, following the Master down the drive toward the home pasture. But as the pack began to stream across the field toward the first covert, the Squire, as impatient as ever for the excitement of the chase, thrust forward and galloped ahead with the rest of the field, leaving his daughter and her companion behind.

The ground was soft after the week's rain and the air unseasonably mild, although it was still so early in the morning. Lucy's earlier worries vanished as, together, they broke into a canter. The sheer exhilaration of her horse's speed and the presence of Charles riding next to her was thrilling. She felt a rush of sheer joy and turned her head to look at him. He rode looking straight ahead, his face composed, his hands on the reins firm and strong. Then, as they reached the top of a long slope, Lucy saw the low fence at the bottom. With her eyes shining with excitement, she turned to smile at Charles. Together, with their horses' manes flying, they raced down the hill and leaped the fence side by side.

He turned his head toward her, laughing as they broke into a gallop that took them back up the other side. The rest of the field were well ahead of them, but neither of them cared. Lucy could hear the baying of the hounds far ahead in the next field and the sound of the Huntsman's horn. As they reached woodland, they were forced to slow down, bending in the saddle to avoid the low, overhanging branches. Charles went ahead to thrust the foliage aside with his whip, and then, as the path widened, they rode together, side by side. The trees closed around them, the air filled with the scent of the damp earth mingled with the heady fragrance of horseflesh and leather.

Neither of them uttered a word. Lucy was sharply aware of Charles' presence as he rode beside her, of the breadth of his shoulders, of the powerful thighs in the breeches now flecked with mud, of the hands holding the reins with such effortless control. And in that moment, she was filled with a deep contentment, with an intense happiness that needed no words. This moment was, for her, perfection. This was the man with whom she wanted to spend the rest of her life. And as he turned his head to smile at her, she hoped with a sudden, anxious twist of her heart, that he felt as she did.

"Lucy, we must talk." As if he sensed her need for reassurance, he reached across as they were about to emerge from the wood and touched her arm. And then they saw the riderless horse, a gleaming chestnut, cropping the grass beneath the trees and, not three yards away, a figure crouched in a forlorn heap against the trunk of a tree.

"Dorothea!" Charles leaped from his horse and ran to her, and Lucy watched him with helpless admiration. He was so gloriously lithe and strong, and he was kneeling at the girl's side almost before Lucy had dismounted.

Dorothea was deathly pale, Lucy saw when she reached them, the deep graze on her right cheek livid against the chalk-white skin. But it wasn't her pallor that captured Lucy's attention. It was her stricken look as she gazed up at Charles—a look that was, at that moment, impossible to fathom. And then she turned her head away as he bent over her.

"Where are you hurt?" he asked.

"My ankle," she whispered. "My horse stumbled. I fell awkwardly." Tears started from her eyes as Lucy gazed down at her in sympathetic silence.

"Don't try to talk." Charles stripped off his jacket, slipped an arm around her, and draped the garment around her shoulders. Far from bringing her comfort, the gesture only seemed to make her tears flow faster, but when he offered her his handkerchief, she took it and pressed it to her face.

Lucy glanced at the delicate boot protruding from the voluminous skirt of her riding habit.

"Has she broken her ankle, do you think?"

"No! Surely not!" Lady Dorothea gazed up at them with frightened eyes.

Charles shook his head. "It may be no more than a sprain."

He bent and touched the boot lightly, and she gave a shriek of pain. "I'm sorry. I won't attempt to remove it. It will be best to have it cut off when you get home." He looked up at Lucy. "Is there a house or a farm close by?"

Lucy thought for a moment. "Yes. Appledore Farm. About two miles on."

He nodded. "She must be carried home," he said. "There'll be a wagon at the farm."

"No. Don't leave me!" Dorothea said wildly, seizing his arm. "I think I might faint."

Charles hesitated and then looked at Lucy, his eyes inscrutable. "Perhaps it would be better if you went, Lucy. I'm not familiar with the area, and you will probably be a great deal quicker."

"Are you sure?"

"Yes." He gave an ironic little smile. "She will be quite safe with me." He straightened up for a moment. "Take care," he said, and he pressed her arm as he helped her into the saddle.

"Of course."

Her last view of them as she looked back along the path suffused her with an emotion she had never felt so strongly before. It was jealousy, pure and simple. As she rode out of the woods and raced through the fields toward Appledore Farm, she found herself wishing it was she who had fallen from her horse and hurt herself. It would have been worth it to have felt his arm around her and to have heard his voice soothing away her pain.

When the manservant brought in his copy of the *Times* at breakfast the following morning, Charles, preoccupied by the previous day's events, left it unopened at the side of his plate. His world seemed to have shrunk to the measure of Lintern Magna, and one of its inhabitants in particular, and he was not much interested in anything else.

Lucy had ridden straight back to the Manor after arranging for help at the farm, and he regretted not having had the chance to see her home. Instead, he had felt obliged to accompany Lady Dorothea back to Hardwicke House. The doctor had confirmed an ankle sprain, which would heal within days, and apart from a bruised face, she had suffered no further ill effects.

"I am much obliged to you, sir." James Wyatt had thanked him civilly enough, but his eyes had been hostile, and Charles knew why.

He had ridden home, disappointed at the outcome of a day that had begun with such promise.

"Terrible thing, this shipwreck, sir," Thomas said as he poured his master a second cup of coffee. "Many drowned, they say. The vessel went down in less than ten minutes."

"Shipwreck?" Charles, frowning, reached for the newspaper, and read the headline on the front page.

WRECK OFF THE WEST COAST

The *Royal Standard* Lost in Raging Storm

It is our painful duty to record one of the most distressing shipwrecks that has ever occurred in the Irish Sea. On Wednesday, 10 November, in the early hours of the morning, the SS Royal Standard *of the White Star Line was lost off the coast of Anglesey in North Wales.*

The ship, carrying 258 passengers and crew, was bound for Liverpool. It was almost at the end of its voyage from New York and was due in port the following day, when it ran into a violent storm. Amid tumultuous waves, it struck the rocks fifty yards from shore. The vessel was broken into two and sank within ten minutes.

It is believed that as many as forty of the passengers and crew perished as the sea hurled them against the rocks. Many escaped a watery death by clambering up the steep cliffs to safety. Some were able to cling to pieces of the wreckage and managed to reach the shore. It is

thought, however, that the death toll is likely to increase
as bodies continue to be washed up on the beach.

The passenger list together with the names of crew
members is printed overleaf. We apologize for any errors
and omissions that might have occurred.

This tragic event calls forth our deepest sympathy
both for the victims and for the relatives who have lost
loved ones in such dreadful circumstances. Relatives
and friends may apply to the Harbormaster at Holyhead
for the most recent list of survivors.

When Charles had finished reading, he had gone very pale,
and the knuckles of the hand that clutched the newspaper had
whitened. For several moments, he sat motionless as his mind
struggled to take in the details of the story. Surely, he thought
distractedly, there was some mistake. Perhaps he was wrong
about the name of the ship. But even as the idea occurred
to him, he knew that that was not the case. With an effort, he
forced himself to turn to the next page and scan the passenger
list.

The name leaped at him from the page. *Miss Rachel Bar-*
rett, New York. There was no mistake. It was there in black-
and-white. And now, he could only pray for a miracle.

With a swift, almost convulsive movement, he was on his
feet.

"Thomas!" he shouted. "I must leave immediately. I need to
get to Exeter by half past ten to catch the London train."

My dear Lucy,

I had hoped to see you today, but, unfortunately, an
urgent matter has presented itself and requires my imme-
diate attention. I am leaving this morning in the hope of
getting the London train and a connection to Liverpool.

I was sorry not to have had the opportunity to say
good-bye to you yesterday. You will no doubt be pleased
to hear that Lady Dorothea suffered merely a badly

*sprained ankle and a few scrapes, and apparently there
were no other ill effects.*

*I look forward to seeing you when I return. You have
no idea how often you are in my thoughts.*

Please give my best regards to your parents.
                              Yours most affectionately,
                                        Charles

Lucy's fingers trembled a little as she folded up the letter. It
had been delivered by hand by a Ravenscourt servant, and,
fortunately, when Rawlings had brought it to her, neither of
her parents had been at home.

She sighed. So Charles had gone away yet again, and he had
given her no inkling of when he would return. But yet, his
words had filled her with tremulous hope. She was certain that
when she saw him next, he would declare himself, and she
knew, without a shadow of doubt, what her response would be.

Chapter Thirteen

No!" Lucy's eyes were blazing with anger by the time Grace had finished speaking. "It's simply not true! Charles would never behave like that! I won't believe it, whatever anyone may say!

Grace sighed. "You are my dearest friend, Lucy, and I felt I had to tell you. I know how you feel about Major Ryman, but it is only right that you should know what has been said about him."

The two had planned to go for a ride that morning, but the early-morning sunshine had given way, yet again, to drizzling rain, and they had been obliged to sit indoors before the drawing-room fire.

Grace had listened patiently to the story of Dorothea's accident and the part played in it by Charles, and it had been a while before she had summoned up the courage to unburden herself. And now that she had said her piece, Lucy's reaction had been predictable.

"I'm sorry, but I don't believe a word of it. Charles would never behave in that way."

"But Lady Dorothea moved in the same circles as he, and she told Isabel about his shocking behavior only the other day."

Lucy stared at her friend mutinously. "What, exactly, does she say about him?"

"That he is a philanderer. A man who trifles with women's affections and treats them with scant regard."

Lucy's heart was thudding against her ribs. "Impossible! Charles is incapable of such conduct. He has always treated me with the greatest respect."

But despite her fierce denial, there was a tiny, insidious doubt lurking somewhere inside even as she defended him. How could she forget the clandestine meeting in the Rose Garden in Florence? The stolen kiss? The brief moments of passion on the island in the lake? The ardent embrace inside the carriage only the other day?

Grace watched her face anxiously. Reluctant to cause her friend more pain, she hesitated for a moment before plunging on. "There is more that you should know," she said at last. "According to Isabel, Major Ryman has made unwelcome advances to Lady Dorothea. Apparently, he tried to force his attentions upon her when he was staying on the family estate last year in Norfolk." Grace looked away, unable to bear the pain in Lucy's eyes. "And, apparently, as a result, her father asked him to leave."

Lucy was very white, but although her mouth was trembling, her eyes were defiant as she stared at her friend. "I shall believe that only when I hear Charles confirm it. Until then, I don't wish to hear his name blackened any further."

"But, Lucy, even yesterday . . . when you had gone for help, Dorothea said that his behavior was most inappropriate."

"No!" Lucy jumped to her feet, thrusting away the memory of the look she had seen in Charles' eyes when she had left him alone with Dorothea. "I don't wish to hear any more! How can you repeat these things, Grace?"

"I would never dream of telling anyone but you. Surely you know that. But you must see that it is only right that I should warn you. Are you certain of your feelings for him? And, more important, is he worthy of those feelings?"

"Of course he is!" Lucy's mouth set stubbornly, but was there a fearful note in her voice that she was unable to disguise.

Grace took her cold hand in hers. "I know this is none of my business, and please forgive me for asking, but has Major Ryman actually made his intentions clear?"

Lucy looked away. Suddenly, all the fire in her died, and she shook her head. "No. Not in so many words."

"In that case, I would advise caution, dear." Grace's voice

was gentle. "I have no doubt that he is deeply attracted to you. No one who has seen you together could deny that. But until such time that he makes it clear that his intentions are honorable, and speaks to your father, please do not be alone with him. At least, promise me that."

Lucy sat down and turned to her friend. "I know you are only thinking of my best interests," she said quietly. "But you must allow me to use my own judgement—and to bear the consequences if necessary."

But she knew in her heart that Grace was right. Why, after all, would Dorothea have said such things about Charles unless they were true? The accusations of philandering she might have dismissed as idle gossip, but these shocking allegations were far more serious. How could she possibly be in love with such a man? And what would her father have to say when he heard these latest revelations?

And yet, while her reason was telling her to heed Grace's well-meant advice, her heart was still refusing to believe a word against the man she loved. She would not think ill of him until she had spoken to him and looked into his eyes. Then and only then would she know the truth.

The beach was deserted. As Charles stood there on the little gray jetty with the sun glancing off the calm blue surface of the sea, it was impossible to imagine the terrible scene that had taken place here at St. David's Bay only a few days earlier. The only reminders of the broken ship and its passengers were a few broken spars and some grotesquely twisted pieces of metal strewn among the rocks at the water's edge.

Charles shuddered and turned away. He could only thank God, he thought, as he made his way back to the village, that Rachel was safe. All through the long journey from Devonshire via London and Liverpool to Wales, he had expected the worst. And his relief and joy had been overwhelming when he saw her name on the survivors' list the Harbormaster had shown him on his arrival at Holyhead.

It was only a short walk to the inn where some of the *Royal*

Standard survivors had been lodged to await transport to Liverpool. And Charles would never forget the expression on Rachel's face as she opened the door of her room and saw him standing there.

"Charles?" She had staggered back a little at the sight of him. Her hands flew to her face, and then, with a cry, she flung herself into his arms. "I can't believe it's really you!"

"Rachel, my dear girl. Thank God you are safe!" He had taken her by the shoulders then, to look at her more closely. Shocked by her pallor, he touched the ugly purple bruise on her temple, took her hands in his, and saw the bandage on her left wrist.

"You are hurt!"

She shook her head. "Hardly at all. Believe me. It is nothing compared to the injuries suffered by others, and I am fortunate to be alive."

He followed her into the little room with its sloping beams and uneven floor and drew her down to sit with him on the window seat.

"I was afraid to hope," he said. "Afraid even to look at the list of survivors. So many lost! And most of them women and children!"

Her eyes filled with tears. "Several of them had become my friends. The voyage had been so pleasant, so uneventful. We had no idea of what lay ahead."

He took her hands gently in his. "It must have been terrifying."

"When the ship broke in two, and I found myself in the water, I was sure I would drown. If it hadn't been for the brave sailor who came to my aid, I would not have survived." She shuddered. "Somehow, he managed to lash me to a spar, and we reached the shore together. Truly, Charles, I am grateful to God for sending him to help me. He vanished even before I had time to thank him."

He nodded. "If I can discover his whereabouts, I shall make sure to reward him."

Later, as they sat together over a simple meal prepared for

them by the innkeeper's kindly wife, Rachel told him of the sheer horror the passengers and crew aboard the *Royal Standard* had endured.

"I have never felt so frightened," Rachel whispered, her eyes filling with tears as she recalled the terrifying events. "It was such a dreadful storm. I was thrown from my bed by the tossing of the ship in the middle of the night, and when we went on deck, the waves were mountainous. We were all certain we would die. They tried to lower the life rafts, but it was impossible. And then, when we struck the rocks, the ship began to break up, and we were thrown into the sea."

Charles put out his hand and covered hers. It had been almost a year since he had last seen her. She was thinner than he remembered, and her slight form was enveloped in a plain black muslin gown that seemed to be several sizes too big for her. There were dark shadows under her eyes, and there was no doubt that the ordeal she had suffered had taken its toll. Rachel had lost her sparkle. But he knew that she had a reserve of inner strength that would help her to recover and regain her lost confidence.

"You have had a terrible experience," he said gently. "And it will not be easy to put it behind you. As soon as you feel strong enough, we will leave for London, and then you may begin your new life."

"But I have lost everything! All my possessions!" Rachel said. "Money. Papers. My books. Everything I had brought with me. The clothes I am wearing were given to me by one of the ladies who came to help. I have nothing, only the garments I was wearing aboard ship that night, and they are now little more than rags."

"Leave everything to me," Charles said gently. "Nothing matters now except that you are safe and well. Once we have gone through the formalities with the shipping line, I will take you to Liverpool, and we can try to replace some of the things you have lost."

"You are so kind to me."

He shook his head. "It is only what you deserve."

As soon as Rachel was safely ensconced in the rooms he had taken for her in London, he thought, he would return to Lintern Magna and make a full confession to Lucy. He knew he could no longer go on leading a double life. The arrival of Rachel had made his choice very clear.

"Mr. James Wyatt to see you, Miss Lucy."

Lucy's heart had leaped into her throat when she had heard the sound of male voices in the hall, and when James was announced, she was filled with disappointment. It had been almost two weeks since Charles had left. She had no idea when he would return, and, despite Grace's words of warning, her heart yearned for the sight of him.

What on earth, she wondered, was James doing here?

When he came into the room, she forced a smile. "James! What a surprise!"

He advanced toward her with an expression on his face that Lucy could not fathom. "I'm afraid I waited until I was sure your parents would be out. They're having tea at the Vicarage, I believe."

"Yes, they are." Lucy stared at him blankly. Her parents would never again feel very kindly toward James, and he would not have been particularly welcome. "Is something the matter? You look rather worried."

He sat down next to her on the sofa and looked at her anxiously. "I have something to say to you, Lucy, and I'm not sure how to put it." He gave a rueful smile. "I know what you must think of me. And I don't blame you. I treated you badly, and I behaved like a fool and a bounder."

Lucy shook her head impatiently. "Oh, James, that is in the past. I told you so at the ball."

"I don't deserve your forgiveness." James looked at her searchingly. "But what I want to tell you is this. I have made a terrible mistake. Two mistakes, actually." He swallowed hard. "The thing is . . . well, I'll come straight out with it. The first was not marrying you, and the second was becoming engaged to Dorothea."

There was a long silence as Lucy's face first registered amazement and then alarm. She moved a little away from him on the sofa and clasped her hands together in her lap.

"You see, I don't love her," James said fiercely. "I never did. And I don't think she cares much for me. Which is a good thing, isn't it?"

Lucy, still shocked, shook her head in bewilderment. "What on earth do you mean?"

"I mean that she won't much care when I break off our engagement."

Lucy stared at him, wide-eyed. "James! You don't mean that, surely."

"I do. Absolutely."

"But you can't!" Lucy was outraged. She did not care for Lady Dorothea, but, having endured a similar fate, she would not have wished that kind of suffering upon her. "That poor girl . . . your parents . . ."

"I should never have listened to them in the first place. It's you that I love, Lucy." He seized her hand. "It has always been you. And I was a fool to let you go, when all the time . . ."

Lucy snatched her hand away as if she had been scalded. "James, please! This is appalling! Please, don't go on . . ."

"But it's the truth! Surely you see that. When I wrote you that letter, I thought it was for the best. Your background . . . your history. My parents were totally opposed to the match. I hoped that when you went away, I could stop thinking about you. And for a while, I did. But then, when I saw you at the Hunt Ball with that bounder, Ryman, I knew I couldn't let him take you away from me. I knew—"

"James! Stop this at once!" Lucy was on her feet, backing away, her face pale and her eyes sparkling with contempt. "I won't listen to you a moment longer."

"You must!" He leaped up and tried, once again, to take her hands in his. "I love you, Lucy! I can't help myself. I want you to come away with me! We can elope to Gretna Green, and once we are married, my father will come around. I'm certain of it."

Lucy put her hands behind her back and looked up into his eyes. She was very calm, very composed, and when she spoke, her voice was perfectly steady. "Listen to me, James," she said. "What you are asking is utterly absurd and quite out of the question. And I believe that when you think about it sensibly, you will see that. No!" She put up her hand to silence him as he began to speak. "Please, hear me out. I am fond of you, James. And I always will be. But what I feel for you has never been more than affection between friends. I know that now. You were right to end our friendship, albeit perhaps for the wrong reasons. But I am very glad that you did."

His face crumpled. "You don't mean that!"

"Yes," she said. "I do. Please don't break off your engagement on my account, James. Because I am quite sure that Lady Dorothea will make you much happier than I ever could."

There was a silence as they went on looking at each other, and then James gave a bitter little smile. "It's that blackguard, Ryman, isn't it?" he said. "Well, I hope you know what kind of man he is. I can assure you, everyone else in the neighborhood does!"

Lucy threw him a contemptuous look. "Personally," she said, "I am not in the habit of listening to scandal and gossip. My family has suffered too much from that kind of thing to give it much credence. You see, until the truth proves me wrong, I prefer to make up my own mind about people."

"Really?" James was white with anger. "Then perhaps I should help you to do so. No doubt you would be surprised to learn that on my visit to London last week, I happened to see Ryman at Claridge's. He was dining with a young lady, and, judging from their behavior, it was quite clear that they were more to each other than mere acquaintances."

Lucy felt the color drain from her face. It was as if she had received a very hard blow to the chest, and she was obliged to catch her breath. For a moment, she was quite unable to speak, and then, with an effort, she gathered herself and found her voice.

"Really? And what, exactly, has that to do with me?"

"Only you know that," James said coldly. "But for your own sake, I would advise you not to become involved with a man of his kind. After all, as you pointed out, your family has already been the subject of scandal. It would be a pity to add to it."

Lucy's color was flooding back into her face, and she met his glance without flinching.

"That was not worthy of you, James," she said quietly. "Please go. I have better things to do than to listen to your spiteful remarks."

He took a step away from her, his face working with anger and disappointment. "I'm sorry to have wasted so much of your valuable time," he said bitterly. "I wish you good fortune with Major Ryman. Believe me, you will need it!"

And then, before Lucy could make a reply, James had made her a perfunctory bow and left the room, slamming the door behind him.

"How could I have been so foolish?" Lucy looked at her friend with eyes filled with misery. "I should have listened to you, Grace. You were right to advise caution."

She had fled to Grace, grateful to be able to unburden herself. Her stepmother, she knew, would have been both kind and sympathetic, but she hid nothing from her husband. And still, even after the latest revelation, Lucy could not bear her father to think ill of Charles Ryman.

Grace looked at her with sympathy. "Please don't blame yourself! He is handsome and charming, and he set out to attract you. It was good of James to warn you. After all, he has nothing to gain. It is just a measure of his regard for you."

Lucy opened her mouth to tell her friend exactly why James had come to her but quickly changed her mind. The situation was complicated enough. Grace would be shocked at James' outrageous suggestion, and it was best if she kept it to herself.

"Well, I am better off without Charles Ryman," she said bleakly. This was the second time she had been disillusioned about a man she believed she could trust, and the pain she now felt was far more acute.

"On the face of it, yes. And, judging from all that we have learned about him, it looks as if you have had a narrow escape." Grace looked at her friend anxiously. "When he returns, promise me that you will have nothing more to do with him."

"Perhaps," Lucy said miserably, "he will not be returning at all. He obviously has a reason to stay in London—if what James said is true."

"Do you doubt that?" Grace looked at her with concern.

Lucy shook her head. "No, not at all. Even James would not invent that."

She had left Grace with a heavy heart and had gone home filled with misery. How could she have been so wrong about Charles Ryman? Why had she stubbornly refused to heed Grace's advice, when all the time the truth was staring her in the face?

Only last week, when she and Charles had discovered Lady Dorothea in the woods, it would have been obvious to anyone else that there was something between them. The looks that had passed from one to the other, the use of their Christian names. And surely it would have been more appropriate for Charles to have gone himself to fetch help. But, instead, he had deliberately sent her to the farm so that he could be alone with the woman he had once tried to seduce. Lucy's face burned at the thought, and her anxious state of mind brought on a headache.

She felt so much worse as the day wore on that she could not endure the thought of going with her parents to the carol service, and Adeline, seeing how distressed she was, did not insist upon it.

"What is amiss with Lucy?" her father demanded, as they left in the carriage "She does not normally complain of headaches."

"I think it is more to do with her heart than her head," Adeline said and sighed. "These rumors in the village about Major Ryman have upset her very much."

"Idle gossip, if you ask me. I admit I had my doubts about the fellow when he first arrived here. But I've had no cause to think ill of him."

"True enough."

"And I hear he went to the aid of James Wyatt's fiancée when she took a tumble in Breecher's Woods a couple of weeks ago. Seems a decent enough fellow to me."

"Indeed."

But Adeline was certain that her stepdaughter knew more about Charles Ryman than she was as yet willing to share and wisely said no more on the subject.

After her parents had left, Lucy went downstairs and, to Rawlings' dismay, sent away her dinner without even attempting to eat a morsel of it.

She went to the library and stared at the leather-bound volumes, hoping to distract herself from the thoughts that were causing her so much pain. And when she found a copy of Charles Dickens' *David Copperfield*, which had always been one of her favorites, she curled up in her father's armchair and began to read. From childhood, books had always been a comfort as well as a pleasure, and the familiar words immediately began to weave their spell. But she had not quite finished the first chapter when Rawlings appeared in the doorway, looking none too pleased.

"Major Ryman has called, Miss Lucy. I informed him that your parents were not at home, but he said he needs to speak to you urgently."

Charles followed him into the room almost before he had finished speaking.

"Lucy!" He advanced toward her, hands outstretched. "Forgive me for calling on you so late. I have only just arrived back from London, and I couldn't wait to see you."

Lucy jumped to her feet, her book falling, unheeded, to the

floor and she retreated toward the fireplace. The hot color that had run up into her face quickly receded, and she struggled to maintain her composure. But at first, in his eagerness to speak to her, Charles seemed oblivious to her reaction.

"I meant to write," he said, "but there is so much to say that I thought it better to wait until I saw you." He stopped, frowning, suddenly aware of the look of shock upon her face. "You are well, I hope. You look a little pale."

"I am quite well, thank you."

"Then come and sit down with me, won't you?" he said. "I have been thinking about you constantly, and I can't hold back my feelings a minute longer." He drew closer to her and tried to take her hand. "Don't be afraid," he said. "I have come to tell you how very much I love you. But I think you already knew that."

Lucy's eyes widened. She stared at him in utter disbelief, unable to utter a word, so completely astounded that she allowed him to take her hand.

"I want you to be my wife, Lucy," he said. "But first, before I speak to your father, I have certain things to explain to you. Please hear me out."

The words, spoken so bluntly, so utterly without embellishment, brought Lucy to her senses. She snatched her hand from his fiercely. "I'm afraid," she said, her eyes filled with scorn, "I have no desire whatsoever to hear what you have to say. I wish you to leave. Immediately."

Charles' eyes widened. For a moment or two, he appeared to be completely at a loss. There was a silence so perfect that the ticking of the ormolu clock on the mantelpiece seemed preposterously loud.

When he finally spoke, his voice was unsteady.

"I'm sorry. I have obviously been deluding myself. I thought the feeling between us was mutual."

"It might have been," Lucy replied, "if your conduct had been honorable."

His head came up sharply. "My conduct? Forgive me, but I have no idea what you mean."

"Oh, please," Lucy said curtly. "Don't pretend that you don't know what I am talking about! Do you really think that I would ever be tempted to accept a man who behaves in such a despicable manner?"

"I take it," he said quietly, "that you are referring to my past?"

Lucy stared at him furiously. "I know nothing about your past. The present is bad enough, surely!"

Charles looked at her, his eyes very clear and steady, his face pale under the tanned skin. "I'm afraid," he said quite calmly, "I have no idea what you are talking about. I think you had better tell me clearly what I am guilty of. And, at least, give me the chance to defend myself."

"Very well, then." Lucy's cold smile of contempt did not reach her eyes. "You may recall writing to tell me about your urgent need to be in Liverpool. Perhaps you could tell me why, in that case, you were seen in London, dining alone with a young woman, with whom you were clearly involved."

He nodded, serious-faced. "I can easily explain that. In fact, I came here today with that express object in mind."

Her mouth twisted scornfully. "Really? And were you then going on to explain why you tried to seduce Lady Dorothea when, at the time, you were enjoying her father's hospitality in Norfolk?"

"Who was it told you that?" Charles was suddenly furiously angry, hot color staining his face, and Lucy gave a scornful laugh.

"That is not important. Even more recently, when she was injured during the hunt, your behavior was apparently quite inappropriate. And now the whole village is aware of it!"

He shrugged, his face set. "That is of no consequence to me. What does concern me is the fact that the only woman who truly matters to me should be willing to believe such slander."

He gave her a glance that would remain for a long time in her memory. "I would never have believed that you, of all people, would think so badly of me." He bowed. "I am extremely sorry," he said, "to have imposed myself upon you. I assure you, I shall not trouble you again."

Lucy watched him leave the room, and she heard him bid Rawlings good night. And then, in a state of complete misery, she stole up to her room and cried her heart out.

Chapter Fourteen

Lucy woke, heavy-eyed and heavy-hearted, the following morning after a disturbed and restless night. Her stepmother had looked in upon her when she returned from the Rectory, but she had kept her eyes firmly closed and pretended to be sound asleep. Her pain was still too raw for her to feel able to share it.

She could hardly believe that everything she had hoped for had vanished. Part of her wished for a few, fleeting seconds that she had known nothing about Charles' conduct, but she quickly dismissed the thought. She could only imagine the torment she would have suffered if she had gone blindly into marriage with such a man.

She went down late to breakfast in an effort to avoid the rest of the family and was still sitting there, deep in gloomy thoughts, when her stepmother came into the morning room and handed her a letter.

"This was delivered by one of Major Ryman's servants. He must have arrived back yesterday."

Lucy's hand trembled as she took the square white envelope, and she was of two minds whether to read it in front of her stepmother. But there was little point in hiding the truth, and she drew out the single sheet of paper.

Dear Miss Ashleigh,

I very much regret the abrupt manner in which I left you yesterday. I feel that I should have at least made an attempt to answer the accusations you leveled at me, but in the heat of the moment, my feelings got the better of me, for which I apologize.

There have been incidents in my life of which I am not proud, but I assure you that the charges you laid upon me last night are both without foundation. The first, that I am romantically involved with the young woman I was seen dining with in London, is complete nonsense. I have no idea who this witness was, but I can assure you that my relationship with the lady is absolutely innocent. Miss Barrett is my ward. I became her legal guardian when she was orphaned at the age of eleven. It was my intention, last night, to explain the exact circumstances to you, but obviously there is now no point in doing so, as you have made your feelings toward me very clear.

Miss Barrett recently arrived in this country to train as a nurse at the Florence Nightingale Hospital, and I was in London to arrange suitable accommodations for her until she begins her training in January. I had intended to introduce her to you when she arrives to visit me at Christmas.

The second offense, which I find far more malicious and damaging, refers to my relationship with Lady Dorothea. I can state categorically that on no occasion have I attempted to take advantage of the lady or to jeopardize my friendship with her father by the means you have described. At no time has there been any suggestion of impropriety on my part. Whether you believe me or not is, of course, for you to decide.

It is, I know, impossible for me to refute these lies, and I have no idea where they originated. But I am certain that if you were to approach Lady Dorothea, she would readily endorse my innocence.

I ask you, most humbly, to believe that my intentions toward you were strictly honorable, and I hope you can find it in your heart to accept that.

If not, I doubt that we will meet again, so please accept my best wishes for your happiness in the future.
I remain,

Respectfully yours,
Charles Ryman

When Lucy had finished reading, her cheeks were on fire, and she folded the letter up with shaking hands, quite unable to meet her stepmother's eyes.

"Lucy? What is it? What has he said to upset you?"

Lucy shook her head distractedly. She felt utterly confused and ashamed of herself.

"He has said nothing wrong. Only I think . . ."

"Yes?"

"I think I have spoken out of turn." She covered her face with her hands. "I have said things I should never have said, and now . . ."

"Lucy, dear, I think you had better tell me what has happened." Adeline sat down next to her stepdaughter and put her arms around her. "I'm sure it cannot be as bad as you think."

"Oh, it is, Mama." She looked up, her dark eyes filled with misery. "Last night, Charles . . . Major Ryman told me he wished to marry me. He was going to speak to Papa. And I sent him away . . ."

There was a long silence.

"You must have had good reason to do that, my love, surely," Adeline said at last, her voice very calm and soothing.

"No. I was wrong." And then, with a look of utter dejection, she let the whole story come tumbling out.

Lucy did not attempt to spare herself. "I said some dreadful things. I accused him of deceiving me. Of being a liar and a flirt. You see, James completely misunderstood. I should never have listened to him."

"James?"

"Yes. He called yesterday." Lucy did not wish to upset her stepmother any further by telling her about his proposal to elope to Gretna Green. "He told me that he had seen Charles in London with a young woman . . ."

She thrust the letter into her stepmother's hands. "Read it for yourself. Then you will understand how I feel."

When Adeline had finished reading, she was silent for a few moments. Then she folded up the letter and replaced it in its envelope. "I will say this," she said. "Although I am not well acquainted with Major Ryman, I do not believe him capable of such ungentlemanly conduct. And if he is willing for you to approach Dorothea on the subject, I feel he must be telling the truth."

"But why would Isabel Hardwicke tell lies about Charles? She hardly knows him."

Lady Ashleigh looked thoughtful. "Isabel has a tendency to exaggerate, I can tell you that," she said. "In fact, it was a deliberate exaggeration on her part that once caused a rift between your papa and myself." She smiled a little grimly. "She has never made a secret of her animosity toward us. I don't think, Lucy dear, that she has ever quite forgiven us for taking your father away from her."

Lucy stared at her mother almost eagerly. "So you think Charles is innocent of wrongdoing?"

"Yes, I think so. But there is one thing in this letter that disturbs me. Since Major Ryman has a ward, why has he never mentioned her to you?"

Lucy shook her head. "I have no idea, Mama."

"That does worry me. We know so little about him. In fact, he seems to be at pains to keep his background a secret."

"But, Mama, we do know that he has had a distinguished career as a soldier."

"Yes. But even so, I feel that there is something he is hiding from you. What are these mysterious circumstances he refers to in his letter? Why not explain them there and then?"

Lucy shook her head.

"Are you going to tell Papa?" she asked apprehensively.

"Yes, dear. I must. You know that, don't you?"

Lucy's shoulders drooped. Her hopes, which had been so

encouraged by her stepmother's calm good sense, were once again in tatters.

She went upstairs to her room and stood at the window, looking out over the parkland. The sun was glittering on the frost-covered fields, and the sky was cloudless and blue. All the beauty of her beloved home was there before her, just as it always had been. But for once, Lucy was blind to it. A dark cloud had descended, obscuring its loveliness. And the future had never seemed so bleak.

Chapter Fifteen

Charles, what a wonderful journey it has been! The English countryside is so picturesque. The tiny villages with their little thatched cottages, and those beautiful old churches."

Rachel Barrett, glowing with excitement, had alighted at the station where her guardian was waiting for her. Charles was glad to see that she had recovered from her ordeal and now looked as bright-eyed and cheerful as ever. She was no beauty, but she had an expression of great sweetness, and the goodness of her nature shone through. Charles was very proud of her.

"I'm sure I could see the battlements of a castle as we left Exeter," she said excitedly.

"That would probably be Powderham Castle," Charles said. "It is the home of the Earl of Devon and was built, I believe, in the thirteenth century. I'm told it has been in the family for five hundred years."

"Really? That is so fascinating! With all these wonderful places to see, it is no wonder that you have stayed in this part of the world for so long." She took his arm and smiled up at him as they followed the porter along the platform. "Tell me, when shall I meet Miss Ashleigh? I'm so looking forward to it."

During his stay in London, Charles had confided in her about Lucy; he had explained how he had met her and had told her of his intention to ask her to be his wife. Rachel had been delighted for him and eager to make her acquaintance.

But now, his smile was forced, and he did not reply to her question.

"Here's the carriage," he said, and he took her hand to help her in.

And she was so enthralled by everything she saw as they drove to Ravenscourt House that her guardian's somber mood went, temporarily, unnoticed.

Refreshments were served immediately after her arrival. It was Rachel's first experience of the traditional afternoon tea, and she enjoyed sampling everything: the cucumber sandwiches cut into tiny triangles, the crisp wedges of toast thick with yellow butter, the fluffy scones filled with strawberry jam and clotted cream, the iced cake sitting on a silver salver, the milky tea served in fragile Wedgwood cups.

Afterward, they went to sit by the fire in the library, and it was then that she noticed how withdrawn Charles seemed.

"You don't seem yourself," she said, suddenly anxious. "Is there something wrong? Are you quite sure I'm not imposing on your hospitality?"

"I'm very happy you are here," Charles said. "The truth is, I had been looking forward to introducing you to Lucy Ashleigh. But now, that is not possible."

Rachel looked across at him in surprise. "Really? Is she not at home?"

Charles was not normally in the habit of unburdening himself to anyone. But one of the main reasons for Rachel's visit to Lintern Magna had been for her to meet his prospective bride. He knew he had no alternative but to explain what had transpired between himself and Lucy. She laughed when he told her what James Wyatt had inferred when he had seen them dining together. But the accusations leveled at him relating to Lady Dorothea filled her with disgust.

"How," she asked, outraged, "could anyone imagine you to be guilty of such conduct? And who could be wicked enough to spread such lies?"

"I have no idea."

"But the whole thing is utterly ridiculous."

"To you, perhaps, it is. Because you know me so well. But sadly, small villages are often slow to accept a newcomer, let alone trust him. And a foreigner, to boot!"

"But surely, Miss Ashleigh knows you better."

Charles sighed. Rachel's forthright honesty was sometimes hard to bear, and it pained him to admit that she was right.

He shrugged. "These places are alive with gossip, and rumor can sometimes be mistaken for the truth. Also, Lucy once had an unhappy experience, which would make it very hard for her to trust someone like myself."

Rachel looked across at him, her eyes very direct. "Do you really love her, Charles?"

"Yes. I do."

"Then why are you not prepared to do something about it? Go to her—tell her that she must believe in you. That you are meant to be together and that nothing must keep you apart."

He shook his head. "I wrote to her," he said, "over a week ago. I am still waiting for a reply."

"Oh, Charles!" Rachel reached out and touched his hand. "Don't give up hope yet."

"I think I must," he said. "My lease is up at the end of January. And then I plan to return to London to see you before returning home."

Rachel searched his face. "It's unlike you to give up so easily, especially when you know that right is on your side."

He smiled ruefully. "Unfortunately," he said, "I have not been entirely frank with Lucy about my rather regrettable past. I guess it's too late to unburden myself now."

Rachel shook her head. "It's never too late. And I feel sure that your Lucy will understand."

He covered her hand with his. "I am glad you are here, Rachel. And you must not worry about me. I shall do my best to make sure that you enjoy Christmas. After all you have been through, you deserve it."

Christmas morning dawned cold and bright, with a scattering of snow on the ground. Lucy would infinitely have preferred not to attend church, but today, of course, it would have been impossible to avoid it. Her father was reading the lesson, and the whole family would attend.

As she dressed, her head was throbbing after yet another broken night's sleep. She felt infinitely sad. Ever since her father had brought her, when she was ten years old, to live at the Manor, Christmas had always been such a joyous time. But this morning, not even the heady, resinous scent of the huge tree in the Great Hall could lift her spirits. The children had helped their mother to decorate it the day before, and as Lucy walked slowly down the staircase to breakfast, she remembered all the other times the mere sight of it, with its gaily wrapped gifts and softly gleaming candles, had filled her with joy.

"Why are you sad, Lucy?" Antonia slipped her arm through her sister's as they rode in the carriage to church. "It's Christmas Day! After church, we can open our gifts."

"Yes," said Harry. "And we are having roast goose for dinner."

"And plum pudding with a sixpence inside it!" Piers added. He regarded his older sister critically. "Why are your eyes red?" he demanded.

"I'm just a little tired, that is all," Lucy said, and she turned to stare out the window.

"It's probably because she's been crying," Harry informed his brother, rolling his eyes. "Girls do that all the time."

Piers made a face. "Why are they such crybabies?"

"Girls are not crybabies!" Antonia, outraged at such slander, stuck her tongue out at her brothers.

"Oh, yes, they are," they chorused, grinning. "Crybabies! Crybabies!"

"Enough!" their mother admonished them as her small daughter's lips began to tremble. "Tell them what little girls are made of, Antonia."

"Sugar and spice and all things nice!" she said, brightening. "That's what little girls are made of!"

"And what are little boys made of?" their mother asked them.

"Snips and snails and puppy-dog tails! That's what little boys are made of!" they shouted, to Antonia's delight. And then they proceeded to make hideous faces and yelping sounds until their father, who was riding outside on the box beside the coachman, roared at them.

"Behave yourself, you ruffians, or you'll get down and walk the rest of the way!"

Lucy sighed. There were times when, dearly as she loved her sister and brothers, their noisy energy drove her mad.

The bells were pealing out joyously as the Ashleighs trooped into the church, which was filled with the scent of winter greenery. Great swathes of ivy twined around the pulpit, with holly and mistletoe trailing from the lectern and choir stalls. Before the chancel steps, the great stone urns spilled over with scarlet poinsettias and Christmas roses.

As usual, on this festive morning, the little church was full. As Lucy took her seat next to her stepmother in the family pew, she glanced across the aisle to smile a greeting at Grace and Philip, who were seated with Lord and Lady Hardwicke. Behind them in the Wyatt pew were George and Isabel. And on the far side of James and Dorothea was a stranger, a burly figure with a shock of white hair and a full beard.

"Is that Father Christmas?" said Antonia in a loud stage whisper, and Lucy exchanged an amused glance with Adeline as she bent hastily to quiet the excited little girl.

It was as Miss Waite took her place at the organ to play her favorite Christmas piece from Handel's *Messiah* that Lucy became aware of a sudden stir behind her as the church door opened, letting in a blast of cold air. When she glanced over her shoulder, she froze at the sight of Charles Ryman making his way down the central aisle with a tall, dark-haired young woman at his side.

This, of course, must be his ward. Lucy's face went hot when she remembered how bitterly she had spoken of her. Already, she found herself desperately plotting to find a way to escape at the end of the service so that she would not have to come face-to-face with either of them.

The booming voice of the rector, as he began the service, did little to calm her wildly beating heart. In the choir stalls, she could see her young brothers, angelic in spotless surplices and scarlet cassocks, singing the opening carol with gusto. But when she opened her mouth, no sound emerged, although she knew the Christmas hymns by heart.

The familiar words uttered by the vicar fell on deaf ears, and her fingers shook too much to turn over the pages of her prayer book. But when her father left his seat and strode to the lectern to take his place behind the brass eagle, she forced herself to concentrate.

"Here beginneth the second chapter of the Gospel according to St Matthew. 'Now when Jesus was born in Bethlehem of Judaea in the days of Herod the King, behold, there came Wise Men from the East . . .'"

There was something infinitely comforting about the sound of Papa's deep voice as he read, something so utterly reassuring about the sight of his upright, stalwart figure, that Lucy immediately began to feel calmer. And by the time the service ended, she was able to smile at the vicar, now standing by the west door, and wish him a Merry Christmas.

Her plan was to hurry down the path to the carriage to wait for the rest of the family. But as she was about to set off, Grace, who was in conversation with her mother, motioned to her to join them. And as she reluctantly turned back, she came face-to-face with Charles Ryman and his ward as they emerged from the church.

They were too close for her to try to avoid them, and she stood her ground, willing herself to appear calm.

"Major Ryman." Her lips were so stiff that it was an effort to speak.

He bowed. "Good morning, Miss Ashleigh. Merry Christmas." He was, she saw by his expression, as affected by the confrontation as she was but equally determined to observe the civilities. "May I present my ward, Miss Rachel Barrett?"

Lucy looked into a pair of candid brown eyes and forced a smile. "I am happy to make your acquaintance, Miss Barrett."

There was warmth in the smile she received. "I have been so looking forward to meeting you, haven't I, Charles?" Rachel said, without a trace of affectation. "And you are every bit as lovely as he said you were!"

Blushing hotly, Lucy stood back as Charles introduced his ward to the others. Miss Barrett's open, friendly manner did much to ease the rather stilted conversation that ensued, and they were just about to part company when a burly figure stepped forward.

"Good Lord!" The strident voice turned heads. "Charles! Charles Ryman!"

Charles bowed. "Lord Fitzallan!"

"My dear fellow! What brings you to this part of the world? I thought you'd returned to New York."

"Not until the New Year."

"This is such an unexpected pleasure!" He seized Charles' hand and pumped it up and down. "Dotty!" He turned to his daughter, who hung behind, looking as if she wished the earth would swallow her. "Why in the name of heaven didn't you tell me Charles was in the neighborhood?"

Lucy, now walking with Grace and her stepmother toward the carriages, was not the only one to be shocked by the significance of the little scene.

"And Lord Fitzallan is supposed to have asked Major Ryman to leave his house," Grace muttered in disgust. "I'm so sorry to have repeated such a falsehood, Lucy. Surely Isabel could not have made the story up!"

"It might not be entirely of Isabel's invention," Lady Ashleigh said. "She may have misunderstood something Lady Dorothea mentioned."

"But why did Dorothea look so guilty?" Lucy asked.

"I have no idea," Grace said. "But I intend to find out. In fact, I shall ask Isabel myself."

"I must say, I liked Miss Barrett," Lady Ashleigh said. "She seemed to be a very pleasant young woman."

"She is, indeed," said Grace. "And so brave! Did you know that the ship she traveled in across the Atlantic sank in a terrible storm off the Welsh coast and that she almost lost her life?"

They stared at her in amazement.

"Oh, yes, Major Ryman told Philip about it. He went to Anglesey to meet her and found her in a dreadful state!"

"How terrible!"

Lucy was horrified. The memory of the angry accusations she had flung at Charles seemed now to be even more shameful. And in the carriage on the way home, prevented from discussing the matter further with her stepmother in front of the children, she stared out of the window across the frosty fields, barely aware of the excited chatter all around her.

Torn between relief that Charles was so clearly innocent of wrongdoing and remorse that she had ever thought him capable of such behavior, she knew it was too late for regrets. He had been scrupulously polite but had barely glanced at her. She did not blame him. She was sorry for every unkind thought she had allowed herself to have. And the friendliness and courtesy of Miss Barrett had filled her with shame.

When they arrived at the Manor, the carriage door burst open, and the children tumbled out.

"Merry Christmas!" they shouted as they flew upstairs to take off their things. "Merry Christmas, everyone!"

The delicious smell of roast goose pervaded the air, mingled with the scent of pine. Even the shining suits of armor lining the paneled walls were garlanded by greenery, and in the vast fireplace, flames were roaring up the chimney.

At last they were all seated at the long refectory table, and the pale winter sunlight streaming through the mullioned windows set the crystal glasses and silverware gleaming.

There was a great basket of fruit as a centerpiece, and gold crackers framed each place setting. And when Rawlings carried in the goose on its silver salver and set it before the master of the house, Lucy looked at the eager faces of the children and remembered that this was their day.

She caught her father's eye and smiled at him. Today she would not let her own troubles spoil the occasion. She would keep the thoughts of Charles far back in her mind until she was alone. And so she joined in the laughter and chatter around the table and exclaimed over her gifts with the others and afterward played the children's games—Blindman's Bluff and Hide-and-Seek, followed by charades—with every sign of enjoyment. Only her stepmother understood the effort Lucy was making, and her heart ached for her.

Lucy did not appear for breakfast the following day, and when, heavy-eyed, she finally came downstairs, Adeline was struck by her pallor.

Her father appeared not to notice.

"You're not hunting, Lucy?" He was clearly disappointed to see that she was not wearing her riding habit. The Boxing Day Meet, traditionally hosted by Lord Wyatt, was one of the most popular events of the year. "But why? You came last year and thoroughly enjoyed the run. And it's such a fine morning. Change your mind and please me, won't you?"

"I'm sorry, Papa," Lucy said. "I had meant to go, but I feel rather tired this morning."

"I'll come with you!" Piers hung on his father's arm, his dark eyes gleaming with excitement. "Please take me, Papa!"

Guy Ashleigh shook his head and gave his son a gentle cuff. "In two years' time, I may consider it."

"But I'll be eleven next year, and I'm a better rider than Lucy! You know I am! Why can't I hunt with you, Papa?"

"Because your legs are not strong enough yet."

"But I could handle Spirit! You know I could!"

His father laughed. Spirit was his best hunter, an Irish thoroughbred, appropriately named. "He'd deposit you in the first ditch, you young braggart!" But his eyes were full of pride as he spoke.

"It's not fair!" the boy muttered as he marched out of the room. "I am strong enough! I'll show you!"

Adeline smiled. Piers was every inch his father's son—just as plucky and every bit as rebellious as Guy had been at his age. Harry was gentler and more studious, and, as for Lucy? Her stepmother suppressed a sigh.

There had always been something vulnerable about her, no

doubt due to the tragic circumstances of her birth. Those early years spent in the workhouse, when her father had not known of her existence, had left their mark. And although they had done everything in their power to make up for all that she had lost, the shadows of the past would never entirely disappear.

That old, lost look of hers, which they hoped had gone forever, had returned. This was the second time she had given her heart away, and perhaps on this occasion, the damage would not be so easily repaired.

"Mama?" Lucy was staring at her. "What is it?"

Adeline shook her head and forced a smile. "It's nothing. Just a foolish thought. I'm so glad that you decided not to hunt today, dear. Let us go into the morning room and be cozy."

"Have I made you unhappy?" Lucy asked, as they settled down on either side of the fire.

"My dear, of course not. But it pains me to see you look so sad."

"I can't help myself," Lucy said. "Charles hardly looked at me yesterday. Even his voice was cold. And it is entirely my fault. I have ruined everything."

"You are not to blame, Lucy. You had been misled. Besides, you felt betrayed by James, and once that happens, it is not easy to trust again. Once, before I married your father, I allowed myself to believe an untruth about him, and I ran away. And so I know what it is like to lose faith in someone you love. If your great-uncle Roderick had not sought me out to tell me the truth, I would not be sitting here with you today." She took Lucy's hand in hers. "If Major Ryman is meant for you, Lucy, these obstacles to your happiness will disappear, I promise."

But Lucy's smile was far from convincing, and Adeline, trying to think how best to cheer her, was about to suggest a drive to visit Grace, when Rawlings announced an unexpected guest.

"A Miss Barrett to see you, my lady. She apologizes for calling unexpectedly and understands if it is not convenient."

Adeline exchanged glances with her stepdaughter as Lucy, utterly disconcerted, sat up straight.

"Thank you, Rawlings. Please show her in."

Rachel Barrett entered the room with a smile. She was wearing a brown mantle trimmed with fur over a plaid dress, sensible boots, and a plain felt hat. There was a naturalness about her appearance and manner that Adeline immediately warmed to.

"Miss Barrett! What a very great pleasure to see you!"

"Thank you so much for receiving me, Lady Ashleigh," she said. "I know this is most irregular, but you see, as I return to London in the New Year, I shall not have many opportunities to make your acquaintance."

"Not at all," Adeline said. "Please, do sit down."

"Thank you." She took the seat next to Lucy on the sofa and smiled at her. "I wish I was staying longer so that we could have seen more of each other. Charles has spoken so warmly of you."

"Really?" Lucy said, rather faintly. "How kind."

"May I offer you some refreshment, Miss Barrett?" Adeline asked. "Some tea, perhaps?"

"Thank you, but no. I have not yet acquired the English habit of drinking hot tea, although I'm certain I soon will. And in any case, I will not impose myself upon you for very long. Charles has promised to take me for a drive, and as I am leaving next week, I want to see as much of your lovely countryside as possible."

"You are leaving so soon?" Lucy, still struggling to cope with the situation, asked her with an effort.

"Yes. I begin my training on the fifteenth of January at the Florence Nightingale Hospital. But first I go to Portsmouth to stay with a friend I met on board ship. I was so happy to hear from her; I was afraid that she had not survived."

"I hope you have fully recovered from your dreadful ordeal at sea," Adeline said. "It must have been a terrifying experience."

"Yes, it was. But I was one of the fortunate. So many lost their lives, and it has made me feel that I was saved for the very purpose I had set for myself."

Lucy looked at her admiringly. "And how long is the training?"

"One year. I'm told that there are twenty-five students in my class, and I am looking forward to meeting them. We shall wear special uniforms and be instructed by a Matron and her assistants." Rachel's face was animated as she spoke. "The rules are strict, and I have a great deal to learn. I am so grateful to Charles for encouraging me and giving me this opportunity. I have dreamed of becoming a nurse since I was a child."

"And have you met Miss Nightingale?" Adeline asked.

"Oh, yes. She interviewed me in London in her rooms in South Street. I was very honored. She is stern but very kind, and they say that she sends her nurses flowers to welcome them on their first day!"

"What a thoughtful gesture!" Adeline said, looking up as the butler knocked and entered the room. "Yes? What is it, Rawlings?"

"Beg pardon, my lady, but there has been some trouble at the stables. Bates wishes to speak to you urgently."

Adeline frowned in disbelief. "Really?"

"I believe, my lady, it is a serious matter."

"I see." She got to her feet. "Would you excuse me, Miss Barrett?"

"Certainly."

When Adeline had left the room, Rachel turned to Lucy. "I am glad of the opportunity to speak to you alone," she said in her forthright way. "I was hoping to be able to talk to you about Charles. Forgive me if I sound rather blunt."

Lucy, taken aback, colored slightly. "Not at all."

"I know Charles would say it really isn't any of my business, but I just wanted to assure you that there is no truth in any of the rumors circulating about him. They are completely unfounded. My guardian is the kindest and best of men, and he is quite incapable of the kind of behavior he has been charged with."

Lucy looked away. "There is really no need . . ."

"Please, hear me out. Charles is too honorable to speak ill

of a lady, and he wouldn't approve of my interference. But I feel that you ought to know the truth. You see, when he first met Lady Dorothea, she became infatuated with him. He made it clear that he had no interest in her, but she continued to pursue him. Charles felt that he had to leave the Fitzallan estate on a pretext rather than cause her father embarrassment. And he did not set eyes on Lady Dorothea again until they met here, at the Hunt Ball. I'm afraid she invented everything else."

Lucy met Rachel's candid gaze. "I realized that I had been misinformed," she said quietly. "I'm sorry that Charles has been the subject of such slander."

Rachel nodded. "I believe it was one of your poets who said, 'Hell hath no fury like a woman scorned,' isn't that so?" She paused, looking at Lucy as if she was wondering whether to say more. "You may think me presumptuous, but I would ask of you one thing. Whatever you learn about Charles in the future, please do not judge him."

But Adeline was hurrying back into the room before Lucy could reply. "It's Piers," she said, white-faced. "He's disappeared! Bates thinks he has taken Spirit from the stables. He may be trying to follow the Hunt!"

Chapter Sixteen

The head groom stood in the Great Hall, twisting his cap between his gnarled old fingers.

"You are absolutely certain it was Piers who took the horse?" Adeline asked him, forcing herself to remain calm.

"Yes, my lady, I'm certain."

"But I thought Papa was riding Spirit," Lucy said.

"Yes, miss, he meant to. But when I saddled him up, I noticed a wound on his leg, and the Master decided to take Caspar instead."

Seeing the stableman's distress, Lucy gently coaxed the story from him. Piers had been at the stables, grooming Brownie, his pony, when two of the lads had begun fighting.

"It took everybody's attention and three of us to separate the young ruffians. And that's when I reckon Master Piers must have taken Spirit."

"You're absolutely sure it was Piers?" Lady Ashleigh said, her eyes anxious.

"Oh, yes, my lady. Brownie was still tied up in the yard. And the grooming tools Master Piers was using were lying on the ground nearby."

Lucy looked at her stepmother. "He told Papa that he wanted to ride Spirit only this morning."

Bates shook his head. "The young master has good hands and plenty of pluck. But Spirit! That's a tall order, miss, for a lad of his age."

It was dark, and snow was falling when Charles Ryman was returning home after another fruitless search of the fields and woods. When Rachel had arrived home and told him about the missing boy, he had set out immediately to join the search party led by Guy Ashleigh.

Spirit had been found not a mile away in a small copse on neighboring land, but, three hours later, there was still no sign of Piers. The horse had lost a shoe and was limping a bit but seemed otherwise unhurt, and it was thought that the boy must have been thrown. The question was, where?

Concern for Piers' safety grew with every minute that passed.

His father was finally forced to call off the search until first light the following morning, and, heavyhearted, Guy had returned to the Manor. Charles could not begin to imagine what he must be feeling, fearing the worst and faced with the prospect of telling his distraught wife and family that Piers was still missing.

As Charles cantered down the dark lane with the icy wind blowing the snow into his face, he was thinking of Lucy and what she must be feeling as she waited for news of her brother. The sadness of being estranged from her had been dragging at his heart for days. It was the first thing he thought of on waking each morning and the last at night.

He had reached the top of a long, steep lane when the falling snow began to turn into a blizzard, and his mare's hooves began to lose their grip on the icy surface. There was nothing for it but to dismount, and as he peered around for some form of shelter, he saw, not twenty yards away, the shape of a small wooden outbuilding standing in the lee of the hedge. As swiftly as he could, he led the horse toward it. The door, hanging from one rusty hinge, was propped up, leaving an opening wide enough to get through, and the snow was already piling up in the entrance.

Quickly, his gloved hands numb, he tethered the mare to the rusty handle and stooped to enter. As he did so, something stirred in the blackness inside, and he heard a gasp followed by a cry. The next second, there was a sudden rush toward him, and a small, frantic body tried to get between him and the doorway.

Charles' first instinct was to recoil from what he assumed was an animal, but as the creature tried to force his way past, he suddenly realized, with a surge of relief, that he had found the missing boy.

They were forced to wait until the snowstorm had abated before Charles felt it was safe to set out for the Manor.

The boy appeared to have suffered no serious injury, but his lips were blue with cold. His clothes were frozen stiff, and, at first, he was shivering too much to be able to speak coherently.

Charles stripped off his greatcoat and wrapped it around the small, trembling figure and gradually managed to coax the story of his adventure from him.

When Spirit had bolted, an overhanging branch had swept Piers from the saddle, and the resulting fall had stunned him. By the time he had recovered his wits, there was no sign of Spirit, and Piers had spent some time searching for him before crawling into the outbuilding to shelter from the snow.

"The horse has been found. He was not hurt," Charles said kindly. The boy's eyes lit up, and he gave a long sigh of relief.

"Papa will give me a licking for this, though," he muttered through frozen lips, and Charles put an arm around the trembling shoulders.

"I believe you'll find he will be more relieved than angry."

Not long afterward, the wind dropped, and it stopped snowing. And when he had hoisted the boy up in front of him in the saddle, they made their way back to the Manor, where they were welcomed with utter relief and joy.

Lucy rushed into the hall with her parents to greet them. And the two younger children escaped their nanny and came running down the stairs in their nightclothes to hurl themselves upon their brother.

Apart from the briefest nod of acknowledgment, Charles did not look in Lucy's direction until he had handed the shivering boy over to his relieved parents.

"I think he'll do," he said. "Just a few cuts and bruises."

And after he had stripped off his sodden jacket, he found himself in an armchair drawn up to the fire with a glass of cognac in his hands.

Lucy could barely take her eyes off him, willing him to look in her direction, hoping for some sign that he had forgiven her. But he seemed to concentrate his full attention on her brother as the boy explained what had happened.

"I'm sorry, Papa! I thought I could handle Spirit," Piers said from the depths of the blanket in which his mother had wrapped him. "It was fine at first, and we went like the wind. But then a gun went off in the woods, and he bolted."

His father glanced at the ugly bruise on the boy's forehead. "You were lucky, by the look of it, you young scapegrace," he growled.

He looked fearfully at his father. "Spirit's all right, though."

"Yes, no thanks to you. Think yourself lucky he wasn't badly hurt. You'll stay away from the stables until I'm convinced you have learned your lesson. Do you hear?"

"Yes, sir."

When a subdued Piers had gone upstairs for a hot bath and Adeline had shooed the others to bed, Guy turned to Charles Ryman.

"I am greatly indebted to you, sir. I can never repay you—that's certain!"

Charles shook his head. "I am glad to have been of service," he said. "It was by the merest chance that I found the boy. I had given up the search and was on my way home."

"If he had remained in that outbuilding overnight, he might have frozen to death!" exclaimed Guy. "I should have taken a stick to his backside for this piece of tomfoolery! My uncle would have given me a licking for far less."

"Oh, Papa," Lucy said. "All that matters is that he is safe."

Charles nodded. "And I don't believe he will do that again in a hurry."

"You will stay for dinner, I hope, Major?" Guy Ashleigh said.

"Thank you but no." He gestured at his wet, mud-spattered breeches. "I guess I'm not fit for civilized company."

"Another time, then? You must allow me to show my appreciation for your help tonight."

Charles smiled. "I'd be grateful if you'd stable my horse and give me the use of your carriage to get home."

"Of course. I'll tell Rawlings to have it brought 'round at once." He stood and left the room.

Charles and Lucy were left alone together, and there was a long, difficult silence. "Thank you so much for being kind enough to search for my brother," Lucy said at last.

He glanced at her briefly. "It was the least I could do. When Rachel told me what had happened, I knew how anxious you would all be."

"Miss Barrett is charming," Lucy said awkwardly. "I'm sorry her visit was cut short. I barely had time to say good-bye to her."

"I'm sure she understood."

"She returns to London shortly?"

"Yes."

Lucy forced herself to look up into his face. She had to make some attempt to reach him. It was now or never.

"I'm very sorry," she said, her voice trembling a little, "for misjudging you. It was quite wrong of me to think badly of you."

He nodded, but his face was impassive, his voice cold. "It doesn't matter."

There was another silence. There seemed no more to say.

Her father returned to say that the carriage was ready, and they both followed Charles to the door to bid him good night.

"I'll have a groom return your horse tomorrow and retrieve the carriage. Once again, many, many thanks. If ever I can be of service to you, sir, please do not hesitate to call upon me."

"Thank you, sir."

The two men exchanged a warm handshake, Charles touched his hat to Lucy, and they stood watching as the carriage disappeared down the drive into the darkness.

What did you expect? Lucy asked herself bitterly as she went upstairs to her room. How could she have been foolish enough to imagine that he had forgiven her? Charles . . . Charles. His name ached and throbbed in her heart. But there was nothing she could do about it now. She had lost him, and she had no one but herself to blame.

The following afternoon, Grace called with news that had shaken the entire neighborhood and had entirely superseded the exaggerated accounts of Piers Ashleigh's latest scrape.

"Lucy, you will not believe it—the most shocking thing! James has broken off his engagement to Dorothea!"

Lucy sighed. So James really had meant what he said and had ignored her well-meant advice.

"She has already left for London with her father!" Grace said. "I knew little of it until my brother told me last night. There was a dreadful scene after church on Christmas Day when she more or less confessed to having told lies about Major Ryman. And now the whole family is in a state of shock."

"Have you spoken to James?"

"No. But Philip has. He says that his parents are threatening to disown him."

"I'm not surprised," Lucy said. "They would expect him to accept his fiancée's shortcomings."

"Yes, I'm afraid they would. After all, Lord Fitzallan is one of the richest men in England. But I think that if James really loved Dorothea, he would have been willing to forgive her anything."

"Perhaps."

"Philip feels sorry for James. He says the match was forced on him by his parents. And that he was glad of an excuse to break off his engagement." Grace sighed. "They should never have stopped him marrying you."

Lucy shook her head. "I'm very glad they did!"

Part of her felt sorry for Dorothea. She had been rejected by both James and Charles, and the disgrace of the broken engagement would be incredibly difficult to put behind her.

Lucy knew exactly what it felt like to be cast aside, and the whole affair, together with her estrangement from Charles, filled her with despondency. She wondered why love had to be such a painful, difficult thing for her, not in the least like the romantic dreams she had once had.

After Grace left, Lucy remembered that she had promised her mother to help Miss Waite with the church flowers. It was Adeline's weekly task, but she had gone to visit her best friend, Jane Ambrose, who was sick with a fever.

It was the last thing Lucy wanted to do. Miss Waite was notoriously fussy and exacting, but after a nursery lunch with the children, who were strangely subdued after the previous night's excitement, she set off for the church.

There was still a thin covering of snow upon the ground, and the air was like wine, pure and sweet and heady. As she walked briskly along, she indulged in a little fantasy in which she suddenly looked up and saw Charles Ryman coming toward her. All the past constraint between them would have vanished, and at some point—she did not exactly envisage how and where—he would take her in his arms and tell her that he still loved her.

She was so deep into her reverie that she managed to reach her destination without remembering a single detail of her journey there. When she entered the church, she saw that Miss Waite had already begun the task of tidying up the greenery that had strewn the chancel.

"There you are, dear!" Her sallow cheeks were flushed with exertion, and some thin gray wisps of hair had escaped from her bun. "You had better start on the larger urns."

Despite Lucy's best efforts at arranging the flowers, Miss Waite was not impressed. Her faded blue eyes examined Lucy's vases of hydrangeas and chrysanthemums critically.

"Always cut your stem one inch higher than the rim, dear. And please remove those leaves, or they will rot under the water."

And Lucy was subjected to a long hour of advice and instruction, which she endured with admirable restraint.

She was just wondering how she could make her escape

when the door opened, and James Wyatt walked in. She could not mask her surprise as he marched up the central aisle toward her.

"Lucy! Rawlings said I would find you here." He made Miss Waite a defiant bow. "Good afternoon. I have come to drive Miss Ashleigh home. That's if you're finished here?"

Lucy glanced quickly at Miss Waite's shocked face. The old lady was, of course, fully acquainted with all the latest gossip, and her expression said everything. Was there no end to this young man's outrageous behavior?

"I think Miss Waite might be glad to see the back of me," Lucy said with a smile.

"Of course not, dear! Your help has been invaluable." But she let her go without further protest, no doubt, Lucy thought, eager to hurry off to report on the latest scandalous developments.

"I hope I didn't embarrass you," James said, as they walked down the path to the lych-gate.

Lucy smiled faintly. "Not in the least. I was glad to make my escape."

"I suppose you have heard about my broken engagement." He glanced at her defiantly. "I know you don't agree, but I believe that I have done the right thing."

"I'm sorry for you both."

James shook his head. "We don't deserve your sympathy. I should never have asked her to marry me."

He helped her into the cabriolet and jumped up beside her. "Anyway, I'm glad it's over. My only regret is that I was foolish enough to allow my parents to influence me. But it was my own fault. I should never have let you go."

Lucy moved a little farther away from him and clasped her hands in her lap as they set off toward the Manor. "James, please don't. We've already discussed that."

He turned his head to look at her. "I just need to know whether there is any chance that you might change your mind and marry me."

"You already know the answer to that." Lucy clutched the

hand rail to steady herself as the horse gathered speed. "And please, rein the horse in. You are frightening me."

"I'm sorry." He slowed the animal to a walk as they turned into the Manor gates. "I knew what your answer would be, but I had to ask one more time, just to be sure." He sighed. "I shall go abroad for a while. Give my pater a chance to cool down."

"Where will you go?"

"Europe. France, perhaps. Or Monte Carlo. Friends of mine have a place there. It's a good place to winter." He shrugged rather petulantly. "What does it matter?"

"I'm sorry, James," Lucy said gently, moved by the desolate expression on his handsome face. "I know that one day you will find someone who will make you happy."

"I wish I could believe that."

He pulled up on the gravel sweep and helped her down beside him.

"If you ever change your mind . . ." He took her hands, looking down at her sadly.

She shook her head. "Good-bye, James."

He sighed. "Good-bye, then, sweet Lucy." And as he bent and kissed her cheek, the great oak door opened, and Charles Ryman came walking down the steps toward them.

"He had waited for you to return for a good half hour," Adeline said. "I had only just arrived back from visiting poor Jane, and I was certain you would be home at any minute."

"And he definitely wished to see me? Not Papa?"

"Oh, yes. He made that clear."

"Oh, Mama!"

Lucy covered her face with her hands. What must Charles have thought as he emerged from the house and saw her being kissed by James!

"He just stood there on the steps for a few moments. I think he said something about the weather, and James muttered some sort of reply. And then the groom brought his horse around, and he just raised his hat and left." She looked at her stepmother despairingly. "If only I hadn't allowed James to drive me home! Oh, why is everything so impossible?"

Her stepmother sighed. "I believe it was Shakespeare who said, 'The course of true love never doth run smooth.'" She took Lucy's cold hands in hers. "Perhaps it will turn out well in the end. He said that he might call again."

But Lucy would not be comforted. She was certain that he must have thought he had interrupted some kind of intimate scene between her and James. And she felt that her last chance to reestablish her relationship with him had gone forever.

Chapter Seventeen

The New Year's Eve Ball was this year to be hosted by the Hardwickes, and Grace had been busy helping her parents with the elaborate arrangements. Traditionally, guests were expected to wear fancy dress, and it was considered to be the highlight of the county's social calendar.

"I shall go as the Queen of Hearts, I think," Grace confided to Lucy. "Philip, of course, refuses to wear anything but hunting pink. Mama has decided upon Elizabeth I, and I gather Isabel is to be Marie Antoinette." She gave her friend a mischievous glance. "That will be quite appropriate, if you ask me!"

"Yes, indeed." Lucy sighed. "I don't think I will bother to dress up this year. I'm afraid I don't feel particularly festive."

"Nonsense! You must go in a costume like the rest of us," Grace said, looking severe. "I wonder," she added artfully, "what Major Ryman will be wearing?"

At the sound of his name, Lucy looked up from her needlework, her cheeks flushing painfully.

"Charles will be there?"

"He has promised that he and Miss Barrett will attend. He and Philip have become good friends. Philip never believed the rumors and lies said about him. He thinks Major Ryman has been shamefully treated."

Lucy's eyes brightened. "Philip is quite right. When I think of the way I judged and condemned him, I feel very ashamed."

"Well, perhaps you can tell him how you feel at the ball," Grace said airily. "Now, what about your costume? Something Italian, perhaps? I think that would strike the right note."

Lucy gazed at her friend. Suddenly she knew exactly what

she would wear. Everyone who saw the portrait of the Florentine lady hanging above the fireplace in the library at the Manor commented upon Lucy's likeness to her. And when she mentioned her idea to her stepmother, Adeline thought it an excellent plan. Together, they plundered the chests in the attic, where they found a wonderful hoard of gowns and headdresses, family heirlooms long forgotten but as beautiful as ever when they were shaken out and pressed.

And so, on New Year's Eve, Lucy appeared in a costume that turned heads as she walked into the room. She was wearing a gown of richly embroidered brocade and silver lace, which left her graceful shoulders bare and accentuated her tiny waist. The sleeves fell in circles to the wrist, and the full skirt was parted to reveal an exquisite under petticoat.

Her dark hair was swept back from her face and adorned with tiny jewels and surmounted by a pointed cap ornamented with silver pearls.

Seated on the balcony with Grace, who looked every inch a Queen of Hearts, and Philip, resplendent in his scarlet jacket, she gazed down at the brilliant scene below. It seemed to her that practically the entire county had turned out for the occasion, most of them in colorful costumes, dancing beneath the glittering chandeliers.

But Lucy was barely aware of the spectacle or the music and laughter. There was only one person she longed to see, and she scanned the faces of the dancers eagerly. It was impossible to imagine what kind of disguise Charles would be wearing.

A pirate, complete with striped jersey and a red bandana, waltzed by with Maid Marian. George Hardwicke with Marie Antoinette in his arms waved up at her. A tall, fair-haired man in dress uniform whirled past, and for one heart-stopping moment, Lucy thought she had found Charles, until he turned his head.

She knew or at least recognized most people in the room, but as she looked around, her attention was caught by a complete stranger who had a decidedly foreign air about him.

He had an unfashionably luxuriant moustache and wore a

yellow-and-black-brocade waistcoat instead of the conventional white—and an oversized bow tie.

"Who is the tall man talking to your father?" she asked Grace.

"He is an American newspaper publisher. I believe his name is Stryder," Grace said. "Apparently, he's visiting relatives of his in Exeter who have some connection with the Wyatts." She gave Lucy a mischievous glance. "I must say, he's not nearly as handsome as our other American guest, as I'm sure you will agree."

Lucy smiled rather bleakly. Where was Charles? There was as yet no sign of him or Rachel Barrett.

When Philip asked her to dance, she willed herself not to look around the room and forced herself to concentrate instead on the steps of the quadrille.

"I wonder where Ryman has got to?" Philip said, as if he had read her thoughts. "Let me know if you spot him, won't you? He and Miss Barrett are meant to be sitting with our party."

Lucy nodded. She was beginning to believe that Charles had decided not to attend.

But a few minutes later, when she and Philip were returning to their seats, she looked up, and in an alcove just off the dance floor, she saw a tall figure in evening dress standing there alone.

Her heart gave a great leap. He was here! She pressed Philip's arm and motioned him to look in Charles' direction. He looked aloof and unsmiling, but he raised his hand in salute when he saw that she had noticed him.

"There he is at last!" Philip said. "I knew he wouldn't let me down!"

He came forward to join them, and the blue eyes met Lucy's with a warmth that gave her anxious heart hope. The frigid mask he had assumed when she saw him last had vanished, and for a moment, he was the man she had fallen in love with all that time ago.

"Where is Miss Barrett?" she asked him.

"I believe she is dancing with a sailor!" He laughed. "Rather a strange partner for Joan of Arc. But Rachel always believes in entering into the spirit of things."

Lucy was glad that Charles was not wearing some ridiculous costume. Men, she thought distractedly, always looked their best in formal dress, and he was no exception. The white shirt was dazzling against his tanned face, and he wore his evening clothes with an air of casual distinction.

"Come and join us at our table," Philip said.

But the band had begun to play Strauss' "Emperor Waltz," and Charles turned to Lucy.

"May I have the honor of this dance, Miss Ashleigh?"

As if she had been hypnotized, she took his hand and let him lead her to the dance floor.

At first her body felt stiff and awkward in his arms. Conscious of the speculative looks of those around them, she moved like a marionette, jerky and mechanical. But then, as he held her close, she felt her limbs relax. She was achingly aware of him, of his fine, chiseled features, of the way his blond hair curled behind his ears, of the hard strength of his body against hers. His nearness awakened in Lucy a quite shocking sensation of desire, and she knew that he felt it too. They danced as if a spell had been cast over them, so that they were no longer conscious of themselves but merely part of the powerful, compelling emotion that had taken them both prisoner.

"I know exactly who you are," he whispered, his breath soft against her cheek.

"Really?" She gazed up at him.

"You have just stepped down from that beautiful portrait hanging above the fireplace in the drawing room at the Manor."

She gave a little shaky laugh. "Have I?"

"Yes. You are *A Florentine Lady*. Tell me, will you be staying long?"

Her eyes sparkled. "Just for tonight."

"And then?"

"I shall be plain Lucy again."

He smiled. " 'Plain Lucy'? Impossible!"

She met his eyes, and her heart leaped as she saw the sudden longing in them. "Charles," she said, "the other afternoon . . . I want to explain about James. I know what you must think of me, but . . ."

"No," he said quietly, "let us put that behind us. I wish you all the happiness in the world. But I will always remember that the sweetest moments of my life were those I spent with you. And I shall never forget how beautiful you look tonight."

The music died, and she stood looking at him helplessly, searching in vain for the right words. "Charles, please . . ."

But he was already offering her his arm to escort her back to her table.

As they turned, a man's voice, loud and American, suddenly accosted him.

"Well, I'll be damned! If it isn't Charles Ryman!"

Charles turned his head and looked at Edward Stryder blankly.

"I knew it was you, Major!" There was a strange note of triumph in the man's raucous voice. "I never forget a face!"

Charles frowned. "I'm sorry," he said, rather coldly. "I don't believe we have met."

Stryder smiled unpleasantly. "That's so," he said. "We haven't. But I know you, all right. The name's Stryder. My newspaper covered your court-martial."

Lucy would never forget the shock of those words or the scene that followed: the silence that fell after the man's pronouncement, the heads turning from one to the other, Charles standing there, stiff and immobile, as if paralyzed.

Then he stepped forward, fists clenched at his side, eyes blazing with anger. For a few terrible moments, Lucy was quite certain he was about to strike the sneering face of the man who had confronted him. But, somehow, he seemed to get control of himself and stood his ground.

"Yes, sir!" Stryder grinned. "It was quite a scoop!"

"Really?" Charles' voice, a whiplash, rang out. "Then I can only hope that your newspaper reported the facts with some degree of accuracy."

Then, turning on his heel, he took Lucy's trembling arm and led her back to her friends. The shock was visible on their faces. They were aghast. Philip got hastily to his feet to pull out Lucy's chair, and Grace, seeing her distress, reached out to take her hand.

Charles stood before them with the stubborn pride of a man who refused to apologize or to explain. But Lucy saw how white he was, glimpsed the pain in his eyes, and was desperate to shield him from the accusing looks of those around him. She felt absolutely bewildered. Charles? Court-martialed? An officer who had been decorated for gallantry on the field of battle? Edward Stryder must have been mistaken! And yet, if that was the case, why had Charles not attempted to deny the claim?

She looked at him, willing him to tell them all it was a monstrous lie. But he merely made them an ironic bow.

"I'm afraid I must ask you to excuse me," he said quietly. "Good night."

He glanced once at Lucy, and she saw the message in his eyes and knew, with an aching heart, that he was saying good-bye.

As she watched him walk away with that free, graceful gait of his, a great coldness seemed to penetrate her whole being.

Philip and Grace looked at her, desperate to offer comfort, but could find nothing to say. It was Isabel Hardwicke who had the last word.

"Well, now we know," she said almost with relish. "I was always certain the man was a charlatan." She gave Lucy a scornful glance. "He's done nothing but cause trouble since he arrived. We're well rid of him!"

At midnight, as the joyful bells of the parish church rang out and the revelers raised their glasses to celebrate the New Year, Lucy sat alone in a quiet corner of the ladies' dressing room, trying desperately to disguise her burning cheeks and tear-filled eyes.

She had fled from the ballroom, no longer able to listen to the cruel comments that were being made about the man she loved. The story had now permeated the entire room, and it seemed that minute by minute it had been embellished and exaggerated to horrifying proportions. Charles was a deserter! A renegade. He had betrayed his men. He had shown cowardice in the face of the enemy.

But Lucy's heart would not accept any of it.

She had begged to be taken home, but her father felt it would be churlish to leave so early. "But it isn't true!" she said to her father over and over again. "Charles is not capable of such terrible crimes!"

"Whatever Stryder has said about this man," he told her, "and I have yet to be convinced that it is true, is not our affair. Frankly, I would not trust a newspaper hound farther than I could throw him. But unless Major Ryman categorically denies his allegation, there is nothing to be done about it."

Distraught, Lucy had again begged to be taken home, but her father felt it would be too rude to leave yet. And despite the attempts of both Adeline and Grace to comfort her, Lucy was inconsolable.

But when Rachel Barrett found her and sat down in the chair next to hers, she looked so kind and sympathetic that Lucy was deeply grateful for her presence.

Rachel took off her medieval headdress and turned to her. "As soon as I heard what happened, I knew I had to speak to you," she said. "I was not in the room at the time, but I can only imagine how dreadful the whole incident must have been."

Her kind concern caused Lucy's tears to spill over, and she shook her head, dumb with misery.

Rachel took her hand. "You love him, don't you?" she asked in that direct, matter-of-fact way of hers.

"Yes." Lucy's voice was muffled by the handkerchief she held over her face.

"Then you must not let this come between you." She sighed. "I know that he adores you, and I wish he had felt able to confide in you from the beginning." She shook her head. "Poor Charles! The very thing he most dreaded has finally happened. He must be in despair."

Lucy stared at her, sick at heart. "Then it is true?"

"The court-martial? Yes. Stryder was right. It caused quite a stir at the time. And I don't think that Charles will ever, truly, get over it."

"What?" Lucy's voice was a whisper, and she suddenly went so pale that Rachel put her arm around her.

"My dear, he was found not guilty. Completely absolved of blame."

Lucy raised her head. "I knew it!" Her eyes were suddenly wide with joy. "Oh, thank God! I knew he was incapable of the dreadful things they are saying about him."

She clung to Rachel in utter relief, but the girl's expression remained somber. "Yes, of course," she said quietly. "But I have to tell you that there were some who refused to accept Charles' innocence. Some newspapers, Stryder's in particular, suggested that the verdict was unjust and deliberately dragged his name through the mud." She sighed. "Unfortunately, Charles still blames himself for what happened. I believe he always will."

"But why?" Lucy said fearfully, searching Rachel's face. "What was he accused of?"

Rachel shook her head. "You need to hear the truth from Charles himself."

"Please! You must tell me."

"No. I cannot. You see, I was just a child when it happened, and I am not the right person to explain it to you. But"—she looked into Lucy's eyes—"I can promise you this. Charles was wholly innocent of the crime, and I, above all others, would have cause to turn my back on him if that were not true."

"I don't understand."

"Charles will tell you everything."

"So you won't put my mind at rest?" Lucy said despairingly.

Rachel smiled. "I promise you, there is nothing to fear," she said. "But if, as I truly believe, you love Charles, go to him. You see, he has already decided to leave Lintern Magna. He only came here tonight to say good-bye."

"He is leaving? For America?"

"Yes. So if you wish to see him, there isn't much time."

Lucy met the steady, level gaze and nodded. Suddenly she knew exactly what to do.

"I am grateful to you, Miss Barrett," Lucy said. "More than you will ever know."

"Please, call me Rachel. You see, I like to think that one day you will think of me as a friend."

"I think it already!"

Rachel smiled. "I'm so glad to have met you. I am leaving for Portsmouth early tomorrow morning to visit my friend. We are to go together to London to begin our training. And so I must say good-bye." She leaned forward and kissed Lucy's cheek. "You and Charles are meant for each other. Don't let him go without giving him the chance to explain."

Lucy was shivering, not with cold but with excitement mingled with fear that she might be too late.

She had left the house without telling either of her parents. They would, she knew, have put barriers in her way, and who could have blamed them after last night's revelations? But Lucy was determined to follow her heart, not her head, and she had waited, with growing anxiety, for an opportunity to slip away without being noticed.

"Please hurry, William!"

"Yes, Miss Lucy."

The groom flicked the horses with his whip, and the carriage gained speed and hurtled along the narrow, rutted lanes. Lucy, with her heart pounding, was forced to cling to the hanging strap as they rocked from side to side. They fairly flew up the long drive toward Ravenscourt House, but when they drew up outside, it seemed to Lucy that the place had a deserted air.

No smoke came from the chimneys, and the Virginia creeper, robbed of its glorious autumn color, clung like cobwebs to the walls.

The manservant who opened the door confirmed her worst fears. "I'm afraid there is no one at home, miss. I believe Miss Barrett departed early this morning, and Major Ryman left half an hour ago to take the London train." Then, as if sensing her desperation, he added kindly: "You might catch him at the railway station if you hurry. The train is not expected until half past the hour."

Charles glanced at his fob watch and saw that the train to Paddington was already ten minutes late. It was bitterly cold on the deserted, windswept platform, and he walked up and down, stamping his feet to try to keep warm. From time to time, he glanced up at the signal box, hoping to see the wooden arm raised to announce the imminent arrival of the train.

Now that he had made up his mind to leave—and it had been a painful decision—the sooner he went, the better. The melancholy thought that he would never see Lucy again— never hear her sweet voice, never see her smile—was almost too much to bear. But he told himself that he had made the right decision. She would marry James Wyatt; he had been her first love, and whatever was in the past, she still belonged to his world. He would be able to give her what she needed: a beautiful home in this tranquil Devonshire countryside, children brought up in close proximity to her family, a traditional English way of life.

All he had to offer her was the heartache of leaving behind everything she knew and loved, to begin a new life in a foreign land.

There was only one consolation. At least he would never know now what her answer would have been, if he had asked her to share the burden of the guilt he would carry for the rest of his life.

And now, he thought, he was done with Lintern Magna and everyone connected with it. Let Stryder do his worst! They could think what they liked. He could only hope that Lucy would not think too badly of him and remember the brief happiness they had shared.

As he turned yet again to pace down the length of the platform, he heard the signal click into place and saw, far down the tracks, the plume of steam heralding the arrival of the London train.

"Only fifteen minutes late, sir." The fresh-faced young porter pushed his barrow, laden with Charles' baggage, toward the edge of the platform. "That's the best time it's made this week."

But Charles was not listening. He had looked up at the sound of light, hurrying footsteps, and his heart gave a great leap as he saw Lucy hurrying toward him.

"Charles! Please wait!"

He took the hands held out to him and drew her toward him. "Lucy?" he said incredulously.

She was wearing furs, a rich, dark beaver cloak. Her lovely face, framed by the hood, was delicately flushed, and her eyes were as bright as stars.

"I couldn't let you go," she said breathlessly. "Not until I told you that I love you, Charles. I don't care what Stryder said! I don't care what you may have done! And I can't bear it if you go away!"

His hands tightened into a grip that almost made her cry out. And his reply was drowned out by the train as it thundered into the station and came to a halt with a squealing of brakes and a great hissing of steam.

But there was no need for words. He bent and kissed her passionately, scandalizing the passengers staring at them through the grimy windows and filling the porter with delight.

"Will I put your bags on board, then, sir?" he asked with a mischievous grin.

But Charles was looking at Lucy.

"No," she said. "Please take them to the carriage outside."

With her hand in his, they left the windswept platform, and, once in the privacy of the carriage, he took her into his arms.

"I came last night to say good-bye," he said against her cheek. "When I saw you with James, when he kissed you, I knew he had broken off his engagement to Lady Dorothea, and I thought I had lost you."

"He was only saying good-bye. There was never any possibility of reconciliation. I knew that on the day you and I first met." She raised her eyes to his. "Can you forgive me for doubting you?"

"My dearest love, there is nothing to forgive. I am the one at fault. I should have been open from the beginning."

They sat side by side in the carriage, hands entwined, looking into each other's eyes. "Before I ask you to be my wife, I have to tell you about the court-martial," he said. "I had intended to tell you everything when I returned from settling Rachel in London. I was praying that what I had to say would make no difference to your feelings toward me. But, as you know, it wasn't to be."

"Then tell me now," Lucy said.

He hesitated for a moment, trying to find the right words. "It's not a long story," he began, "but it will stay with me for the rest of my life." His voice was low and steady, and he kept his eyes on hers. "When I was a young soldier, I once killed a man." His hands tightened on hers. "The victim was not an enemy on the field of battle. He was one of my own men."

Charles felt her hands tremble in his, but she went on looking at him, and he saw only love and trust in her eyes.

"We had been on the march for three days." The blue eyes were suddenly remote, the voice almost without expression. "When we arrived at Fort Lafayette in New York, the men were exhausted and in desperate need of a rest. That night, I walked in on an argument breaking out over a game of cards. Within minutes, the quarrel became white-hot, and the man accused of cheating drew a gun." He glanced out the window, steadying himself to finish the story. "I ordered him to put the pistol down, and when he refused, I tried to take it from him. In the struggle, the gun went off. I was unhurt, but the man was killed instantly by a bullet to the heart."

Lucy was very pale, but she clung to Charles' hand, and her eyes never left his face. "It was an accident."

His mouth twisted. "Yes, I was exonerated at the court-martial. But if it had been any other man under my command,

I might have behaved differently. He was a few years my senior and had challenged my authority once or twice before. I should never have tried to disarm him, but my pride wouldn't let me lose face before my men."

"It was not your fault!"

"I wish I could believe that." He looked at Lucy with pain-filled eyes. "But for the rest of my life, I will have that man's blood on my hands. It was my pride that killed Sergeant Barrett. And that is the truth."

"Barrett?" Lucy stared at him. "Then Rachel . . ."

He nodded. "His daughter. After the court-martial, I wanted to try to somehow make amends. His family had been left penniless, and I was able to help them. When Rachel was thirteen, her mother died, and I became her guardian." He sighed as if a great burden had been lifted from him. "You know the rest."

In the long silence that followed, Lucy turned her head and stared out the window. It had begun to snow, and large flakes began to settle on the frozen windows of the carriage.

Charles sat with his head bowed, waiting for her to speak and put him out of his misery.

"Charles," she said at last, "why didn't you trust me enough to confide in me? I told you everything about my background. I held nothing back."

"I was afraid that you would be appalled at what I had done. The thought that I might lose your regard stopped me. And even now I believe your father will take a dim view of a man with my history."

Lucy shook her head. "He will understand."

"I very much hope so. But if not, I wouldn't blame him. At home, the case became something of a cause celebre. I lost friends; people I thought were close to me turned their backs."

"In Florence, you said that there was someone once . . . who meant something to you, perhaps?"

"Yes. The notoriety was too much for her and her family to bear."

There was a silence. Then Lucy looked at him.

"Did you," she asked, rather tremulously, "love her very much?"

He smiled. "Until I met you, I never knew what love was. From that first moment when I held you in my arms, on the staircase at the Castello, I have thought of little else but you and my longing to make you my wife."

And the adoration in his eyes as he bent to kiss her was the only confirmation she needed.

Chapter Eighteen

Charles sat in the front pew of St. Luke's parish church, with Eduardo Ortalli at his side. As he waited for Lucy to join him, he felt that he had been preparing for this moment all his life. Her love had changed everything. She had lifted the burden of the past from his shoulders by offering to share it with him.

Guy Ashleigh, arriving at the church with Lucy on his arm, felt the odd mixture of pride and sadness felt by a loving father about to hand over his beloved daughter to the guardianship of another man. When Charles Ryman had come to ask for his permission, his first instinct had been to refuse the request. It was not that he objected to Charles; he had come to respect and admire the man. But the thought of his Lucy leaving for a foreign country thousands of miles away almost broke his heart. To think that he had found this beloved child of his, only to lose her again.

"Lucy must follow her heart," his wife had said, "just as we did."

He knew she was right. Besides, he had already decided that the whole family should visit her in New York as soon as was possible. He had always wanted to see America. And Charles had promised him that not only would there be regular visits to England but that their firstborn would be christened here in this very church.

Adeline, alone in the family pew, waited quietly for the rest of her family to enter. Only ten years ago, she thought, she herself had been a bride, coming, like Lucy, to be united with her beloved. Mingled with the heartache of parting with her stepdaughter was the joy of knowing that Lucy, too, was marrying the man she truly loved.

In the church porch, Lucy turned to smile at her bridesmaids—at Grace's dear, familiar face, at her cousin Sofia, soon to be marrying Eduardo, at Rachel, who had, as she had hoped, become a close friend.

A sudden hush fell over the congregation as Miss Waite began to play Wagner's "Wedding March." Charles, handsome in his dark gray morning coat and white cravat, got quickly to his feet, and a shaft of sunlight turned his blond hair gold. He stood waiting as Lucy began to walk slowly down the aisle on her father's arm. Her beauty took his breath away.

She was wearing a gown of pure white silk trimmed with Milanese lace shot through with silver thread. Her veil was crowned by the diamond tiara given to her by her husband-to-be, and she carried a bouquet of orange blossoms.

Her long train was carried by her young brothers, dressed as pages in dark blue velvet, and she was followed by Antonia, her little flower girl, and her bridesmaids in white muslin frocks tied with broad pink sashes.

As she glided toward the chancel steps on her father's arm, her eyes were fixed upon Charles' face. She had never looked more certain of her love for him. The shadows of the past had fled, and now there was only the joyful prospect of the future.

And when Charles made his solemn pledge before God and all those present "to love her, comfort her, honor her, and keep her, in sickness and in health," he knew that he would be true to this most sacred vow for as long as he lived.

Epilogue

Major and Mrs. Charles Ryman stood on the deck of the RMS *Oceanic*, looking down at the crowds waving hats, handkerchiefs, and flags on the Liverpool quayside below.

Lucy had been both awed and entranced by the beauty of the ship. It was the White Star's first ocean liner and carried 166 first-class and 1000 third-class passengers with a crew of 143.

Their cabin was amidships, away from the vibration of the powerful engines and with the least ocean movement. It had a wide porthole, running water, and an electric bell to summon their steward and was elegantly appointed with mahogany furniture and a four-poster bed. Lucy had been so thrilled with its delights that it had taken all of Charles' powers of persuasion to induce her to go on deck with him for the ship's departure.

"Are you ready to leave England behind, my love?" Charles said, anxiously watching the expression on his wife's face as they stood at the crowded rail.

"Quite ready."

There had been an extremely emotional parting from her beloved family and friends, and he was preparing himself for more tears as they set off to begin their journey to New York.

But Lucy was putting on a brave face, whatever her thoughts, and she smiled up at him as he put his arm around her.

At the expected shout of "All ashore!" friends and relations were making their last farewells, and she was glad that she had dissuaded her parents from making the journey to Liverpool to see them off. The thought of waving good-bye as the great ship slipped its moorings would have been very hard to bear. In this way, she and Charles could set off together, husband and wife, embarking on a journey far more significant than the mere crossing of the Atlantic.

As the *Oceanic* headed out toward the open sea, Charles bent and kissed her lips softly.

"No regrets?" he asked.

She smiled at him with her heart in her eyes. "Not one!"

And as they stood there, at the ship's rail, hand in hand, the shadow of clouds lifted.

The sunlight had never been so bright, nor the future so full of promise.